## "Brace yourself!"

Jasper jerked the wheel hard right, placing himself in the line of danger if they collided. Kinsley's scream seared his eardrums as they spun onto the narrow shoulder.

A *pop pop pop* sent jolts of adrenaline through his veins.

The van was a decoy so the truck driver could get shots in.

"Get down!" He threw an arm over Kinsley's low huddled form, steering them off the shoulder and back onto the road. He pressed the gas and dragged in a ragged breath. The van was a ways behind them now. Only the large gray truck gave chase. He accelerated until they traveled nearly twice the legal speed limit.

"Where are we going?" Kinsley peeked up.

"Away. Stay down." He was pretty sure they were shooting at the tires, which meant they were trying to disable the vehicle to get to Kinsley again. *Why?*

An idea formed. He hated to execute it while Kinsley was with him, but right now there was no choice. He wanted answers about her attackers, and this was the way to get them.

**Kerry Johnson** has been conversing with fictional characters and devouring books since her childhood in the Connecticut woods. A longtime member of ACFW, she's a seven-time Genesis Contest finalist and two-time winner. Kerry lives on the sunny, stormy west coast of Florida with her engineer husband, two teenage sons, eight-year-old niece and way too many books. She loves long walks, all creatures great and small, and iced chai tea.

### Books by Kerry Johnson

### Love Inspired Suspense

*Snowstorm Sabotage*
*Tunnel Creek Ambush*

Visit the Author Profile page at LoveInspired.com.

# TUNNEL CREEK AMBUSH

## KERRY JOHNSON

**LOVE INSPIRED** SUSPENSE
INSPIRATIONAL ROMANCE

# LOVE INSPIRED® SUSPENSE
## INSPIRATIONAL ROMANCE

Recycling programs for this product may not exist in your area.

ISBN-13: 978-1-335-58772-5

Tunnel Creek Ambush

Copyright © 2023 by Kerry Johnson

For questions and comments about the quality of this book, please contact us at CustomerService@Harlequin.com.

Love Inspired
22 Adelaide St. West, 41st Floor
Toronto, Ontario M5H 4E3, Canada
www.LoveInspired.com

**Printed in U.S.A.**

Trust in the Lord with all thine heart;
and lean not unto thine own understanding. In all
thy ways acknowledge him, and he shall direct thy paths.
—*Proverbs* 3:5-6

Dad, you made it so easy to trust in a loving heavenly Father because you were my earthly example. We miss you so much. See you soon.

## Acknowledgments

Kellie VanHorn—thank you for sharing your wisdom and offering lots of encouragement during the writing of this story, and for all those perfectly-timed Baby Yoda GIFs. Let's do this again!

Ali Herring—I'm so glad to be on your team. #ali-ens forever

Dina Davis and Emily Rodmell— I'm grateful for the opportunity to work with both of you. Thank you for your insight and help turning my stories into real live books.

Mom and Mindy— you've kept me afloat in this ocean of grief. I love you.

Jesus—I will follow wherever You lead.

# ONE

Kinsley Miller crept toward Whisper Mountain Tunnel, a prickling sensation climbing the back of her neck. Fireflies winked from the woods, a thousand yellow eyes among the trees. Twilight had settled over Sumter National Forest during her ten-minute hike from the tourist site's parking lot, and night seeped through the trees like spilled ink. There'd be no hikers or sightseers left now. As a wildlife biologist, she was probably the only person in a hundred-mile radius interested in observing the tunnel's tiny nocturnal occupants.

Gray bats.

Kinsley paused mid-step, her shoulders curling forward. Maybe she shouldn't have come out here yet. Her heart sank into her stomach like a stone. Not so soon after Aunt Rhonda's death, at least. But when coworker and fellow biologist Marta had found out Kinsley was taking time off work, heading to her hometown of Tunnel Creek for her aunt's memorial service, she mentioned a colleague's post about rare bats in the Whisper Mountain Tunnel. Marta had encouraged Kinsley to check out the tunnel herself to see if it had been turned into a bat colony.

After all, it'd been decades since the endangered gray bats were last seen in South Carolina. Before she'd dropped her suitcase off at Aunt Rhonda's house, Kinsley headed to the tunnel to watch for them at twilight. *Feeding time.*

So what was this uneasy feeling shadowing her?

Guilt.

That was why she felt uncomfortable. She sucked in her cheeks, pushing through the thick foliage surrounding the man-made tunnel's opening. Guilt because if she'd been here, maybe Aunt Rhonda wouldn't have fallen. Maybe she would've been found earlier, and then… Kinsley closed her eyes to ward off the *what ifs*. The boulder-like blame that had crushed her since she'd gotten the awful call from Jasper Holt.

Jasper. Her high school classmate. Also her ex-boyfriend.

Talk about complicated. The young man she'd loved a decade ago was now a Tunnel Creek police officer, and he'd contacted her with the grim news. The call had been short and shocking, and they'd hung up without discussing a shred of their past.

It'd been a three-hour drive back to Tunnel Creek, each mile colored with images of her once-idyllic life here. If only she'd returned for a visit with Aunt Rhonda before this. She pressed a fist to her mouth as her eyes smarted. Her last goodbye should *not* be a memorial service.

Kinsley swiped at a tear trickling down her cheek, then peered into the fifteen-foot-by-thirty-foot opening. She was here. Might as well check out the area. If the bats had started a colony, they'd burst out of the darkness to feed soon. A spark of joy in her dark, dark night.

A twig snapped. She tensed, glancing into the woods at her back.

Only the sunset's remains stretching orange and pink fingers into the sky met her searching gaze. Tree branches shivered in the light wind, and the distant *drip* of water in the guts of the century-old cavity below Whisper Mountain sent tremors down her limbs.

She shook her head, then adjusted the elastic band of her headlight but kept the light off. Couldn't risk disturbing the colony.

A chuffing sound broke through the branches nearby, almost…human in tone? She choked on a gulp of humid air. Couldn't be. A black bear, maybe? Black bears were docile creatures, unless a sow and her cubs were threatened. Which she wasn't doing.

Silence. She released the breath in tiny increments. Sounded like the animal had wandered off.

She tucked inside the cavernous tunnel and sank to the ground, then located the small silver digital recorder in the outer pocket of her backpack. Seeing the bats leave the tunnel to feed would be incredible. Recording their clicking calls and squeaks would impress Rich, her manager at the zoo, who was a highly regarded chiropterologist and bat conservationist. Maybe it would finally convince him to consider her for lead director of mammals.

*Come on, little beauties.* She drew her legs to her chest as the seconds dragged into minutes.

Kinsley checked her watch.

Why weren't the bats congregating? Twilight was their feeding time.

She rested her ponytail against the cool, gritty wall. Returning to her hometown of Tunnel Creek dredged up memories she'd rather not spend time with. Mom and Dad's accident. Their deaths. Jasper's hurt when she broke off their relationship days before graduation. Running away to college in Atlanta and never looking back.

A branch cracked in the clearing outside the tunnel,

the unnatural racket a red flag. Maybe ten yards away? *That* wasn't the wind.

Her muscles stiffened as she rose to her feet. *Was* it a bear? Couldn't be. They made more noise than that. Could it be a park ranger? Except the ranger station had been dark and locked up when she arrived earlier.

She waited, but the only sounds were the dripping inside the tunnel and the moaning wind.

Her limbs loosened. All the bad memories from her past must've set her on edge. *That has to be it.*

Leaves crunched. Once. Twice. Then, startling silence. Her heart hiccupped as she strained to pinpoint the exact location. She wasn't alone. Someone had followed her.

"I know you're there." A man's voice. Close by. "I've been waiting for you."

Her pulse jammed into overdrive, pounding in her eardrums. *Waiting for me? Why?* She scanned the night sky. Once the moon shone from behind the clouds, could he see her?

An invisible hand held her back from speaking or moving.

Heavy, purposeful steps closed in, like he could see her despite the gray night. Through the descending dark, something shiny glinted in the moonlight. A knife? Kinsley sprang to the right side of the tunnel and took off. She pumped her arms and legs, sprinting toward the hiking path she'd used to come up here. Her car. She had to get to her car.

Footfalls pummeled the ground behind her.

Sharp, shocking pain ricocheted through her skull and neck as someone jerked her hair, holding her back. A scream unfurled in her throat, but she was knocked sideways before it escaped. She flailed for traction, landing hard on the ground. Then hands, fingers, everywhere. Grabbing. Yanking her ponytail, her jacket. She swung the recorder in her hand at him.

"Oh no, you don't, lady." The hot stench of his breath fanned her face, and her stomach roiled in response. "He said you'd be hard to catch in the dark."

"Get off me!" She twisted, one leg sticking out. Her recorder went flying, and her boot struck the attacker's shin. He hissed an oath and let go for a moment. Kinsley wobbled forward, then stood, darting from his reach.

"Where you going?"

*Away*, her heart thrashed out as her body struggled to comply. To move.

Five steps, then ten. But he matched her step-by-step. Then the ground shifted, and she slipped. *No!* Fire burned her scalp as he gripped her ponytail again, slowing her trajectory. A primal cry erupted from her chest. She turned, ramming her elbow into the attacker's ribs, then lifted her knee into his groin. He grunted and crumpled, and she was free again.

"You're going to pay for that!"

Her mind muddled at his words. Who was *he*? Had someone been sent here after *her*?

She lurched forward, disoriented. Where was the path? Branches and stones tripped her, and sticky warmth flowed from her forehead and into her eyes, impairing her vision. Blood?

"C'mon, Kinsley. Tell me where the file is, and this will all be over."

*File?* What did he mean? He knew her name. Why was this happening?

"I don't know what you're talking about!" *Please, God, if You're there, protect me.*

"Sure, you don't." A wiry arm cinched around her waist as her desperate prayer went unanswered. Was he going to kill her?

\* \* \*

Officer Jasper Holt couldn't believe his life now consisted of helping sweet older ladies and their cranky pets while he was off duty. Tonight Elsa Tuttle and her sharp-beaked parrot, Sunshine, needed his help. Talk about a misleading name. Sunshine had escaped in the Tuttle's two-story garage workshop, and catching that feathered monster had required a ladder and *very* thick work gloves.

He shook his head, guiding his Jeep along the familiar winding roads in Sumter National Forest. Thank the good Lord he still had his sense of direction after receiving that brutal head wound last month while on duty. He'd know his way around Tunnel Creek and Sumter blindfolded. That much hadn't changed.

He squeezed the steering wheel until his knuckles cracked. While he hadn't lost his sense of direction, Jasper had gained post-traumatic amnesia and lost something more important: another man's life. His friend and mentor, Park Ranger Willard Tuttle. Mrs. Tuttle's husband. Dealing with Sunshine's beak was the least he could do for the grieving widow.

Jasper released a drawn-out breath. Up ahead, the sign for Whisper Mountain Tunnel jutted out from the trees. The image of Willard's faded blue eyes staring at him, lifeless, from the forest floor replayed in his mind.

Jasper ground his jaw. It was the only detail he could recall from their brutal attack in the woods that day. What he wouldn't give to scrub *that* from his brain and recover the memory of what had happened before he and Willard had checked out that abandoned cabin on the backside of Whisper Mountain, only to find themselves ambushed.

The verse from his bible app cleared the guilt for a

few moments: *He brought me up also out of an horrible pit, out of the miry clay, and set my feet upon a rock.*

But how to get his feet back on solid ground when it felt like his whole world had been rocked by the same weapon that had whacked his skull that day? At least his son was safe. Healthy. Six-year-old Gabe slept at the cabin he shared with Jasper's mom. There was that.

He reached across the console to stroke Dash's big triangular ears. His Dutch shepherd partner sat on the passenger seat, a dog belt latched across his brindle body. "We'll be home soon, boy. Then we'll go for a run."

A quick one. And Dash could do most of the running.

The dog whined and rested his pointed muzzle on the passenger-window glass as they approached the entrance to Whisper Mountain Tunnel. Jasper had given up trying to keep the windows clean.

"Fine. We can just eat, then go to bed. Works for me."

Dash reared back suddenly, letting out a short, sharp bark.

A silver sedan whipped out of the entry road to Whisper Mountain Tunnel, cutting Jasper off. Wheels squealed on pavement. His arm fell over Dash as he slammed the brakes and jerked to the right, entering the road the driver had just exited to avoid hitting them. The car flew past, engine roaring. Jasper started a U-turn to give chase, but a beam of moonlight reflected off a lone car sitting in the lot with one door hanging open.

He jabbed the radio knob on the dashboard transmitter he'd added to the Jeep.

"Linda?"

The dispatcher's voice came over the line. "Jasper, why aren't you home with that cute little man?"

He ignored her teasing and relayed the details about the erratic driver as he drove toward the parked car.

"Whisper Mountain Tunnel parking lot. Silver car. Exited the lot at a high rate of speed. Dent over the back driver-side tire. Dark tint. Couldn't get the plates."

"Oh, hon, it's probably some teenagers putting graffiti in the tunnel, like last month."

Maybe so, but his gut told him it was more than that. "No, don't think so." He squinted as his brights revealed the state of the parked car the moonlight had reflected off of. "There's another car in the lot. Door hanging open. Stuff strewn everywhere but no driver present. This one's a white SUV with Georgia plates. Zulu-Oscar-Zero-Golf-Romeo-Lima-Four-Niner," he read from the plate. "I'm going to check the area."

"Oh dear, Jasper," she cautioned, probably thinking about his last encounter in these woods. "You take it easy. Sending backup—in case."

Jasper thanked her and cut off the call. *You take it easy.* He frowned. Linda never used to say that to him. Only after the incident with Willard Tuttle.

He parked beside the white car, then flicked open his glove compartment and secured his Glock and a flashlight. Unbuckling Dash's doggy belt, he let out a soft whistle. He couldn't rule out that a hiker was lost in the woods, their car burglarized by an opportunist in the meantime.

"Guess we're getting a run in now."

Dash wriggled around the seat in answer, his tail whomping into Jasper as the dog turned in circles. Jasper wasn't the only one who'd missed fieldwork the last few weeks when he'd taken leave to heal from the injury.

*Please, God, keep me and Dash safe.*

He opened the door and stepped onto the pavement. Dash followed with an agile leap. Jasper grabbed Dash's favorite reward—Rocky, an old stuffed squirrel that had long ago lost its squeak—then clicked on his flashlight, the beam of light cutting through the thick darkness. First, he checked the SUV. One door hung open, and the seat belt was tangled in a knot against the door-frame. Numerous items lay on the front passenger seat. Definite vehicle vandalism. Possible stolen items. He shone the flashlight on the back seat, popped the trunk. An open suitcase lay on the ground, a key sticking out of its lock. Clothes and papers flew in the breeze. He commanded Dash to sniff the SUV, his mind opening ten tabs at once. Where was the driver of this vehicle? What other crimes had the driver of the speeding silver car committed?

While the dog worked, Jasper took in the surround-ings. Weren't there property lights in the parking lot? He started forward, Dash at his heel, inspecting the lot. Looking up as Dash sniffed the ground. Sure enough, two light posts stood over the place where the path to the tunnel began. Both lights were dark. Jasper's jaw swung open when he looked down. Bits of shiny parti-cles shone on the asphalt. He commanded Dash to stay, then moved closer and crouched.

*Glass.* Someone had broken the lights. A giant fist compressed his ribs as he stood.

An owl hooted from a nearby tree, then flew off, the whoosh of its powerful wings sending a chill down his spine. Dash lifted his head and scented the wind, whin-ing. Jasper gave wide berth to the glass, keeping the dog close so he wouldn't walk through it.

A branch snapped in the distance, the noise like thun-der in the silence. Jasper peered through the trees on the ridge ahead, his hand glued to his weapon.

Dash sat and whined, his training keeping him in place at Jasper's side. The dog stared at him, trust and eagerness glinting in his dark brown eyes.

"Dash, seek!"

His seventy-five-pound partner was off in a flash of brindle fur and nimble movement. Forest or field or city street, the dog's sure footing and athleticism were levels above his own. Jasper kept the light on his swift form and bounded after him. His heart pounded at the welcome physical exertion and the shot of adrenaline. Finally. It'd been nearly a month with minimal activity. Up ahead, Dash slowed, pacing near a small creek.

Jasper pulled out his weapon and held it across the opposite arm, training the flashlight and Glock on the spot where the sound originated. They were about fifteen feet off the path leading to the tunnel. Signs of a struggle shone under the flashlight's glare. Broken branches. Crushed ferns. Movement to his left captured his attention.

"This is Officer Holt with Tunnel Creek PD. Are you the owner of the white SUV in the parking lot?"

Nothing.

He flashed the beam forward and stepped closer. A dark lump lay in the shallow water. Dash stopped pacing, sitting on his haunches beside the creek. Jasper's stomach sank.

*Please, God, not a body.* Helplessness choked him. Was he too late—again?

Willard's slack features floated through his vision, the blood blooming on the park ranger's chest. Jasper blinked away memories he *didn't* want and hurried forward.

If only he could recall something else about that day. He slowed, snapped his spine straight. Could this situation be related to Willard Tuttle's murder?

A hushed moan carried above the creek's gurgle. Whoever it was, was still alive. *Thank You, Lord.* He rushed to Dash's side, praising the dog, then tossing

Rocky to him. The dog clamped on to the stuffed squirrel, shaking it viciously. Jasper knelt beside the female victim. Long, tangled hair; a trim figure; and hiking boots. Blood matted the side of her head. An assault.

"Ma'am?"

Jasper holstered his weapon, cataloguing the broken ferns and small twigs stuck to her clothes and face. The shallow rise and fall of her chest made *him* breathe easier.

He tugged out his cell. No signal. *Must be in a low reception pocket.* Sumter National Forest had lots of those. Shoving his phone back in his jacket, he addressed the victim.

"Ma'am, I'm Officer Holt with Tunnel Creek PD. Can you tell me your name?"

She moaned again, curling on her side. She wore dark leggings, a long shirt and a windbreaker-type jacket. What was that, a headband? He reached into the tangled mess of her hair, which was lighter than he'd initially thought. Maybe a medium to light brown. It was damp with gritty dirt and creek water. And blood. His flashlight revealed a gash on the side of her forehead, and instead of a headband, she wore some sort of headlight that had slipped over her eyebrows and eyes.

She rolled her head back, muttering indecipherable words. No neck injury, then. When her body shuddered, he set his palms on her arms to anchor her still.

*She must be in shock.* Jasper set up a flare beside her, then commanded Dash to pan out twenty yards. With his faultless hearing, the dog would alert him to any human within a forty-yard perimeter. Jasper tucked the flashlight under his arm and positioned his forearms beneath the woman's body. Couldn't reach dispatch yet. He had to get her to the hospital ASAP.

Cradling her head, he scooped her up and rose. She

felt as light as Gabriel in his arms as he strode back to his Jeep. A startling sense of protectiveness swept over him.

"Jas…"

He froze mid-step. Had she just said his name? *Couldn't have.*

"You're okay, ma'am. I'm right here. You're safe."

Normally, he kept the small talk to a minimum, but something about this woman resonated with him. She reminded him of someone he once knew, but that couldn't be.

The driver of the silver car must be her attacker. His jaw tightened. All signs pointed that way. And while Jasper wanted to catch the man, first he had to make sure she was taken care of so she could give a statement. Then they could track down this perp.

She writhed as he stumbled over the uneven terrain. The headlight inched farther over her eyes, making her look like a grungy, near-drowned pirate.

"Easy. Let's get you to the hospital." He hated to leave the gadget on her face, but what if it had gotten caught in the wound? *The Jeep. Get her to the Jeep.*

Why was she out here now? His boot slipped on a mossy stone. He slid forward but managed to stay upright. She let out a low cry, and he clutched her tighter.

*God, let this woman be okay, please.* He couldn't stand the thought of someone else dying on his watch.

Because he should've been able to stop what happened in the woods that day. He and Willard had hiked up to the deserted cabin behind Whisper Mountain after the park ranger received a tip from a hiker that strange activity was occurring in the area. Instead, Jasper had been knocked out and pushed down an embankment, while the older man had lost his life. Even if Jasper had gotten a glimpse of the killer, the blow to his head had stolen the image.

A tree lay in his path, and he clambered overtop. She let out a whimper when he scaled it, curling deeper into his chest.

"Sorry about that. We're almost there."

"Jasper."

That was his name, clear as a cardinal's cry. Was she one of his sister, Brielle's, friends? Couldn't be. He'd guess her older than Brie's twenty-four but younger than his thirty. Was this someone from town? The hum of a car engine broke through the remaining trees.

Must be his backup. He whistled for Dash, then pushed sideways through the last thickets. Dash heeled as Jasper strode through the parking lot to the Jeep, his gaze following the approaching squad car. Officer Dean Hammond climbed out, his long legs almost twice the length of his upper body. Jasper and Officer Hammond had played basketball for the Tunnel Creek Titans, but only Dean had played college ball at Clemson.

Officer Hammond whistled. "Linda told me to get out here ASAP. What happened?"

Jasper explained the incident with the silver sedan and how he'd found the woman by the creek. He raised his shoulder toward the side of his Jeep. "Mind opening that?"

"I got it." Dean stepped closer, opening the back door. "Did you call the medics yet?"

"No. I didn't have reception back there." Jasper situated the woman on the seat. She curled sideways and murmured into her folded arm as he worked the seat belt carefully over her crumpled form.

"Did you get a look at the driver of the silver car? Plates?"

"Unfortunately, no. I almost hit him when he pulled

out in front of me, and I had to veer in here." He motioned back toward the entry road.

"You didn't give chase, then?"

Jasper blew out a hard breath. "In my Jeep? Takes me five minutes to get to third gear. But then I saw the abandoned car with the door hanging open, and I figured something wasn't right." He gazed at the woman in his back seat. Her hair still covered most of her face, but at least she was moving her arms and legs.

Dean leaned in, eyeing the passenger. "She local?"

"I'm not sure, but she did…" He inched back, then carefully closed the door. No one wanted to be stared at when they were all beat up.

"But she did…" Dean prompted.

"She did say my name when I was carrying her here."

"Whoa, man. You think she *knows* you?"

Jasper shrugged. "I guess so. Maybe she went to Tunnel Creek High? We'll figure it out later."

"Gotcha. You taking her in for questioning, then?"

Dash yipped, nudging Jasper's leg. He swung the front door open, settling the dog in with his belt before turning to face his coworker again.

"First I need to get her to the hospital. She's stable enough that I'll get her there faster than waiting for an ambulance." He thrust a hand through his hair. "I'll get her statement once she's cleared by a doctor. You mind checking out the scene? See if the assailant left any evidence? And that." He pointed to the broken-into white SUV. "I'm fairly certain that's her SUV over there. Someone ransacked it. It'll need to be towed to the station, then checked for prints."

"Sure, I'm on it. I called Matt for backup soon as I saw you carry her out."

Jasper nodded. "I left an orange flare where I found

her beside the creek. Let me know if you find anything."
Jasper gripped Dean's shoulder briefly. "Thanks, man."

"Sure thing. Chief's gonna chew your head off for
doing this yourself."

"I expect nothing less from him." Jasper climbed into
the Jeep and gave Dean a goodbye salute. Chief McCoy
had been overly cautious about Jasper going back to
work after sustaining the head wound. While Jasper
understood his superior's reasoning, it still burned going
from active duty to sidelined for a month.

Not to mention getting coddled like a baby. He hated
that.

He started the Jeep, then gaped in the rearview mirror as his passenger struggled upright. A pair of gray-
blue eyes he would've recognized anywhere collided
with his.

His heart crashed into his ribs. *Kinsley?*

Kinsley Miller. His high school sweetheart—the girl
who broke his heart over a decade ago—sat in the back
seat of his truck, blood drying on her battered face. He'd
known she might be coming back for her aunt's memorial but hadn't expected to see her yet. And certainly
not wounded in his back seat.

A vein throbbed in his temple.

"What are you doing out here, Kinsley?" And who
had attacked her?

# TWO

Kinsley flinched at Jasper's tone. His dog whined, nudging Jasper's right arm. Gone was the friendly teenager she'd been drawn to when they met in home economics. In his place was a steely-eyed police officer—a man now—who clearly wasn't thrilled to see her.

After the way she'd broken up with him and run away from Tunnel Creek at the end of their senior year, she shouldn't be surprised.

Still, his intense stare and sharp question stung. "I'm here for Aunt Rhonda's memorial."

He backed the Jeep out from its parking spot and cleared his throat. "No, I mean what were you doing out *alone* in the *woods*—at *night*?" His eyes bored into hers from the rearview mirror.

"I came a few days early." She carefully removed the headlight from her face and licked her lips, tasting blood. Nausea churned in her stomach. "I was in the woods tonight for work."

"Careful with that. It could provide evidence of your attacker." He nodded at the smashed headlight. "What do you mean, work?"

She squared her shoulders, and the motion sent a fissure of pain down her right arm. "I'm a wildlife biologist currently studying bats. Tracking the colony's movement and feeding patterns. That's it. So why would anyone come after me?"

"Bats. Okay." He drummed his fingertips on the steering wheel, his gaze bouncing between her reflection in the mirror and the road several times. "Probably just an opportunist, but I need to know what happened back there."

She swallowed, her nails scoring her palms, then relayed the minutes leading up to the attack and the attack itself. Her throat closed around the words. "He h-had some kind of walkie-talkie thing on him, and I think another v-voice came on when he was dragging me down the trail." She trembled, shrinking down.

Jasper whistled softly. "It's a good thing I was nearby." He scowled at her again. "But why were you up there at night?"

"I was doing observation work. Bats are nocturnal. They feed at night."

"So do criminals," he muttered.

She continued. "My manager and my department are looking for ways to identify and increase gray-bat colonies in the Southeast. Their numbers are dwindling, which is detrimental to the environment. They're an important insect repellent in our region."

"Really?"

"Yes. They can eat up to one-third of their body weight in insects each night."

"That's…great."

Kinsley frowned. Was he being sarcastic? And did he just shudder?

"So you were here for the memorial but came to Sumter to look for bats."

"That's right."

He checked for traffic before pulling out of the Whisper Mountain Tunnel sightseeing area. "I didn't expect you to be in town yet. And definitely not like this." His sharp tone softened into an apologetic murmur. "I'm sorry I didn't say much when I called about your aunt. Being an officer of the law has its tough parts. Reporting the death of a family member is one of the worst."

"I understand." Her heart plummeted at the reminder of her recent loss. "I think we were both so shocked about Rhonda's death."

He nodded in agreement. "She was a real nice lady."

"She was." Silence highlighted the stressful re-introduction to her high school boyfriend, as well as the ache that grew from speaking about Aunt Rhonda in the past tense.

"Hey, another thing. The white SUV in the parking lot… That's yours, right?"

"Yes." Her car. She'd forgotten about it.

"Someone broke into it, pulled paperwork out of the glove compartment. Opened your luggage."

She flinched, the movement emphasizing every tender point on her body. "That reminds me. The man asked where the files were. I had no idea what he was talking about—still don't."

"Files? Huh. Must have you mixed up with someone else."

"I don't think so." Her chin quivered. "He said my name." Why had *she* become a target?

"So, he knew you. Could it be work-related, by chance?"

"I don't know why they'd want anything from me."

"All signs point to the fact that you have something this person wants. The car has minimal damage. I'll have it towed to the station tonight. Did you have anything valuable in it?"

"My luggage. My laptop. All my things I brought here."

"We need to check for prints first, too. Right now, we're going to the hospital."

"No." She pressed her fingers to her mouth.

"No, what?"

"No hospitals." A deluge of memories threatened to drown her. Sterile white walls and frigid temperatures. Mom and Dad lying so still in matching medical-induced comas, their injuries sustained from the car accident too innumerable to count. The indifferent officer she'd had to recount every awful moment of the accident to.

"Kinsley." His soft, personal admonishment pulled her from the murky swamp of grief. "You could have a concussion."

"Please." She swallowed gingerly, her throat burning from screaming earlier. "Can we go to Rhonda's house first?"

"You really want to go back to that place now?"

"Yes." After Mom and Dad's accident and then their deaths, Aunt Rhonda had moved in with Kinsley so she could finish the school year. She'd encouraged Kinsley to take the scholarship in Atlanta to pursue her degree and her passion for protecting wildlife. She now recognized that her math-teacher aunt had also been mourning Kinsley's father, who was Rhonda's younger half brother, and her sister-in-law. Yet Rhonda had dealt with the aftermath of their deaths, all while urging Kinsley to follow her dreams.

She closed her eyes. Right now, the thought of dealing with painful memories at her old house was less daunting than going to a hospital haunted by her parents' last moments.

And her selfish decisions.

"Please. Just a few minutes. The house is past the Bingham property, off Bradley Lane. Turn left up here."

"I know where it is. What I don't know is why you don't want to see a doctor for that head wound."

She sighed, staring out the Jeep's window. The beautiful forest she'd once loved to explore closed in on them as he drove. "I just can't do it." *Again.*

"Look, I have police protocol to follow. I'm taking you to the hospital."

A sob caught in her throat. "Please, Jas. There's something I want to get at ho—at the house first."

"What do you need?"

Was he angry she used the nickname she used to call him in high school, when life was sweet and their futures were intertwined? Or upset that she refused to comply? Either way, self-preservation kicked in, and she compartmentalized the messy emotions. They always got her into trouble, anyway.

"I need a change of clothes." Aunt Rhonda had kept a dresser full of her old clothes; plus, this way, Kinsley would get a few moments to clean up and gather her thoughts.

He flicked on his turn signal at the four-way stop, and their gazes met in the mirror again.

She broke the eye contact. Had God heard her prayer...and answered it with Jasper?

She hadn't wanted to see him. Hadn't wanted their tangled history to add to the anguish over Rhonda's death. Because if she was honest with herself, she'd been worried he would confront her about their past.

Bring up their heated last conversation, the questions he'd flung at her.

*Why are you doing this, Kinsley?*

*My parents are gone! I need to leave Tunnel Creek. Start over.*

*You don't need to.*

*I do, Jasper. I can't stay here.*

*Please. Don't pull away. I'm here for you. Can't you see that?*

All of it would resurrect the pain she'd been hiding for the last decade.

"Did you tell anyone where you were going?"

His question tugged her back to the present moment. "A couple of my coworkers. But I didn't give them specific days or times."

"The man could've tailed you. You live in Atlanta now, correct?"

"Yes." Had someone followed her into Tunnel Creek? She hadn't been on the lookout for that, so there was no way to know for sure.

"I'll be taking your official statement after the doctors check you out. Let's revisit that then. I'll need names." Jasper spread his right arm across the console, scratching his dog's large triangle-shaped ears. Kinsley smiled when the dog—Dash, if she'd heard correctly—leaned into him with a canine sigh.

"Aunt Rhonda said you got married a few years ago."

In the rearview mirror, his expression shifted. Locked down. Regret coated her tongue like a sour ball. She'd never been great with interpersonal social skills and clearly still wasn't. "Never mind. I shouldn't have said anything."

"No problem. Yes, I did. We got divorced a couple

years ago and she…" He blew out a long breath. "She died recently."

"Jasper, I'm sorry. That sounds difficult."

"Difficult. Yeah, it was." He ran a hand down his face. "So, where exactly are these bats you were looking for?"

She carefully rested her pounding head against the seat. "In the tunnel."

"Come again?" The Jeep lurched slightly.

"A coworker received a tip from a friend who hikes in this area. He'd been on the trail in Sumter and claimed to see bats leaving the Whisper Mountain Tunnel."

"Do you have the friend's name?"

Kinsley squinted against the throbbing inside her skull. "No, just what my coworker Marta said."

"I'm fairly certain there aren't any bats in that tunnel."

"Have you ever looked specifically for them?"

"Why would I do that?"

That was most definitely a shudder. "And do you know everything about Tunnel Creek?"

"Matter of fact, I make it my business to know just about everything around here. When someone sneezes, I say, 'Bless you.' When someone adopts a kitten from the shelter, I go over with catnip and treats. When someone gets married, I send a Tupperware set."

"You do not." She rolled her eyes. Only Jasper would joke at a time like this. "And that just sounds nosy."

"As an officer of the law, it's my job to be nosy."

Despite her stress, despite the pain, warmth unfurled in her chest at his lighthearted humor. And something else—pride? He'd struggled in school with dyslexia, and his grades reflected that, even though he was bright and had always excelled at sports. He'd been one of the friendliest students at Tunnel Creek High, despite his dark good looks. Kinsley blinked. What a couple they'd been, shattering the high school cliché. He'd barely made Cs while carrying the basketball team to state three years in a row, was elected Homecoming King; she'd been on the debate and science teams, maintaining straight As throughout her four years at TCH while avoiding the popular girls and their cliques.

"Just a quick stop, got it?" He turned onto Bradley Lane. "And do me a favor—don't change. We'll need those clothes for evidence. Grab new clothes, then we leave for the hospital ASAP. You can change there."

"But—"

"If you want to stop here, follow my rules. I'm not exactly following protocol here."

She blew out a breath and nodded. "Okay. I'll hurry."

The vehicle cut through the darkness, passing the only other house on the street before reaching the quaint Cape Cod–style house she'd grown up in. She gritted her teeth at the bumpy spot in the road and the feelings that being in this place evoked. *Home.* The house her attorney dad had purchased when she was a baby. A yard in which she'd searched for skinks and watched caterpillars turn to butterflies. Counted cardinals and listened for bullfrog croaks in the pond out back. Her chest constricted as a slideshow of memories played through her mind.

He parked, and Kinsley unbuckled, avoiding looking at the double window on the garage's second floor. Her dad's office. The space he'd used for Miller & Landry, the law firm he and a friend founded several years before his death. How many times had she navigated those stairs to ask if he wanted to join her for a hike in the woods or to tell him about the animal she'd learned about in science class? The pain of his absence chipped away at her heart.

"I haven't been back here in almost a decade."

He turned, eyebrows arched. "You never visited your aunt?"

She straightened her posture. "I was in school for almost six years, volunteering at the wildlife management center near Atlanta. Taking part in multiple animal rescues and studies across the country. Plus, tagging and tracking research trips before I started at Southeastern Zoo in the—"

"Hey—" he held up a hand "—it's your life. I'm just surprised, is all."

"I was always busy with school projects and then work, so she'd visit me." After retiring from teaching a few years ago, Aunt Rhonda would drive down with one of her friends a couple times a year. They'd stay at Kinsley's apartment, then shop downtown. "She kept some of my clothes here because she hoped I'd break down and finally come for a visit."

"But you didn't."

"No." *I couldn't.*

He didn't say anything in judgment as he climbed out of the Jeep. That was a relief. When he opened her door and offered his hand, she willed her legs to work and ignored the pounding in her head. His wide palm gripped her hand; then his other hand caught and cupped her elbow. Careful, proprietary. Once she was upright, he let go and stepped back as though he didn't care to stand within five feet of her.

Jasper had filled out in the years they'd been apart. While he was a lanky six one his senior year of high school, his shoulders had broadened and his voice deepened in the years since, making him a commanding presence and likely an intimidating officer.

She glanced at his profile. Once, she'd loved him with everything in her—the naive adoration of a shy teenage girl who worshipped her outgoing, handsome boyfriend. He'd pulled her out of herself, made her laugh when she was focused on studying the world around her. But nothing good had come of their relationship—least of all her arguing with her mom and dad about where the relationship was headed. Her parents had wanted her to focus on school, not on boys and dating.

They'd liked Jasper, but Mom and Dad wanted to see her get out of Tunnel Creek and achieve her dreams. Become a biologist. Work at a zoo. Looking back now, Kinsley acknowledged that perhaps their expectations guided her decisions more than they should have.

Which didn't matter now. Because she was happy in Atlanta. Fulfilled. And like Jasper and her relationship, that was all in the past.

She ran her palms down her thighs. After her parents' sudden deaths, she'd honored their wishes. Broken it off with Jasper a month before prom, told him she was headed to college in Georgia after graduation and didn't want anything—or anyone—holding her back. Said there was no chance for reconciliation, even though they'd discussed attending the same college and getting engaged in the near future.

Now the words haunted her. As did the wounded, shocked expression he'd worn that day. But she'd used his hurt as decision fuel, adding it to the guilt from her parents' accident, which had given her more justification to leave and start over in Georgia.

She looked from Jasper to the Jeep, where Dash sat

in the front seat, his eyes glued to his master. "Your dog can come inside, too."

"Dash is okay out here, since you'll be quick, right?"

Kinsley nodded, the movement stretching the skin and the cut on her forehead. She released a pained breath.

"We should've gone to the hospital first." He came alongside as she hobbled into the breezeway area.

Near the door, she reached back, then froze. "My backpack. I—I'm not sure where it is."

"There wasn't any pack or bag on or near you. I'd assume your attacker took it."

She mashed her lips together. "But it has my binoculars and field notes in it."

"There's an officer investigating the scene. If he finds the bag, it's evidence. You'll get it back after we're done with it."

She gulped in air. Her wallet was in there, along with the key to her parents' house. She peered around the covered walkway. "There should be a hidden key in the flower bed somewhere…" She crouched, glad to be turned away from him, because her head felt like a freight train had rammed into it when she dropped to search. She wobbled, then caught herself. There. A small, round gray stone—that wasn't really a stone— sat in the overgrown garden area.

She fumbled withdrawing it, then stood to fit the key into the lock. Stars pinpricked her peripheral vision. Jasper's warm hand steadied her arm as she opened the door, and they slipped into the small mudroom connecting the garage to the main house. A thousand memories assaulted her: The smell of Mom's blueberry muffins in the summer and the sound of Dad's boisterous men's group from church. The *click* of their rat terrier, Henley's, nails on the wood floors. The low, tight tone of her parents arguing…about her future, her dad's job, whether to move closer to the city.

"Do you need a light on?" Jasper motioned toward the large room to their left. The kitchen. Even in the dark she could make out the white cabinets with clear glass fronts, the silver fridge, the huge farmhouse sink Mom had chosen when they remodeled.

He flicked on the lights. "Whoa." Stretching out an arm, he stopped her.

Kinsley gasped. Dishes were strewn around the floor, broken into pieces. The cabinet glass was cracked, and the table upended. A chair sat in front of the kitchen cabinets as though someone had climbed on it to check inside. Tipped-over cardboard boxes lay by the back door, paperwork strewn over the tile like spilled candy.

"Jasper? What is this? Aunt Rhonda was a meticulous housekeeper."

"Looks like someone was looking for something." He pulled out his cell and took several pictures. "I'd call this a pattern."

"Do you think this happened recently?"

"Not too recent." He stepped up to the fridge. "Look at this." Jasper crouched, pointing out a jug of orange juice on its side. The sticky liquid spread over the floor in an orange puddle, but it appeared dried out. "I'd guess this stuff's been out for two, three days."

"When Aunt Rhonda…" She gulped like a fish flipped out of its tank.

"The house wasn't torn up. Meticulous, like you said. There was no sign of foul play."

Kinsley sucked in her cheeks to ward off the sting of tears. She hoped Rhonda hadn't suffered, although the fall down a steep flight of wood stairs had proved deadly for her seventy-three-year-old aunt.

He finished taking pictures, then appeared to send a text. "Where are the items you need?"

"Upstairs, in the third bedroom." Her old room. Could she do this? *Had to.* She made her way around the mess, toward the stairs.

Jasper caught up. "I can get the clothes."

"No, thank you. I'm fine."

"Now hold up. Let me check the house."

She pivoted to face him, then grabbed the banister when the room spun.

He was at her side in an instant, holding her upright with his large, gentle hands. "Take it easy. All I need is you passing out and falling."

"I won't pass out." *Hopefully.*

"The door was locked when we came in here, correct?"

"Yes." The word slipped out as her mind ticked through the reality of this dire situation. "Could this be the same person who attacked me at the tunnel? They…came here, too, but earlier? Yesterday, maybe?"

"Appears that way." He strode around the downstairs, checking windows and doors. Tugging on curtains and eyeing the floor. "I don't see a forced entry. I'm going to call this in and get another officer out here to check the property. Sure you don't want me to get the items upstairs?"

"Jasper—"

"I know, you're fine." He cocked a brow. "Two minutes. Just don't touch anything. I'm breaking all sorts of rules here, Kins."

"Okay, okay."

He retreated to the kitchen area; then she turned to face her ghosts.

Kinsley mounted the staircase, avoiding the landing where Aunt Rhonda must've… She gulped, veering around it. Family pictures followed her up each step, beckoning from the wall.

She paused to catch her breath.

Through the banister facing the back window, movement caught her eye. Out in the garden area. Her muscles stiffened as she peered that way. She blinked several times, waiting. *Nothing.* Just the wind playing through the branches of the overgrown red cedar Dad had planted when she was seven.

Had the blow to her head caused floaters in her eyesight? *Must have.*

She gripped the railing and climbed the rest of the way. After reaching the landing, she paused. On the right were two bedrooms and a bathroom. To her left, Mom and Dad's bedroom door remained shut. Her heart withered. She'd barely stepped foot in their bedroom since the accident. She couldn't bring herself to do it now, either.

She headed right. Her old room was now the guest bedroom, and darkness seeped out from underneath the closed door. Two faded yellow night-lights at either end of the hall provided enough light that her hunched-over shadow led the way. Kinsley squared her shoulders and pushed through the door. Moonlight broke through the curtains, spilling across the queen-size bed. Her senior picture and the last family picture of Kinsley and her parents stared out from the same silver frames Mom had given her in high school. She looked away.

She stepped deeper inside the room, tracing the yellow-and-green quilt. Shadows danced around in the corners, chasing away the sweet nostalgia of this space. A spark of unease zinged down her legs, bouncing up to prickle the back of her neck.

"You can do this." She whispered.

She was skittish from the attack at the tunnel—and now from the torn-up kitchen at her old house. All totally understandable. Her body was still in shock. But Jasper was downstairs, and Dash was outside. There was no reason to be fearful.

Kinsley made a beeline for the closet, which covered most of the length of one wall. Inside was a three-drawer dresser, in which Aunt Rhonda had said she'd left Kinsley's shorts and tops.

She grasped the knob and pulled, then registered hangers and scattered clothes on the ground just as a human-sized figure burst from the back of the closet. A sweaty hand covered her mouth, holding her scream captive as they fell backward onto the edge of the bed.

"Tell me where the file is, or it won't end well for you."

His sweat coating her lips roiled her stomach. She lunged across the floor, but he was right behind her, grabbing her like a lion playing with a gazelle.

"The file! We know you have it."

"I don't know what you're talking about!"

"Liar." The intruder's other hand found her throat, and stars dotted her vision as he gripped her neck in a vicious vise. She clawed and kicked to no avail.

*God, help me!*

"Jasper!"

She drew one knee up high and jabbed him—anywhere. She missed his groin but must've hit something sensitive because he groaned and his grip loosened. Kinsley twisted away, rolling across the throw rug. Air. She needed air.

The loose rug swished her forward, knocking her into the bed frame. Queasiness plagued her from the impact and the fast, jerky movements. Her fingers bumped something thin and hard underneath the bed—some sort of folded-up plastic.

Gritting her teeth, she yanked it out. The folding chairs dad had used for their home bible study. She swung it hard at the attacker's shin then shouted for Jasper again.

The seat part of the chair connected with the man's upper legs in a sickening thud. He let out an ugly oath, then stumbled back into the wall.

He pushed off, advancing. *So fast.* She felt like a mouse cornered by a hungry cat. What could she do? Even in the murky light, there was no mistaking the evil glint in his eyes.

He held out both hands and flexed them like he couldn't wait to use them to inflict pain. "Come on! Where is it?"

A loud thump reverberated through the kitchen. *Kinsley.* Jasper fisted his cell, rushing into the living room. He drew his gun and took the stairs two at a time. A scream shattered the home's interior, followed by Kinsley yelling his name. How had an attacker gotten in? A second-story window? Had he already been inside when they arrived?

He should've gone upstairs with her.

On the second-floor landing, he followed the sound of a struggle to the end of the hall. A man's voice shouted a question. Jasper kicked open the door, weapon ready as he assessed the scene. Kinsley cowered beside the bed, a large man hovering over her. The assailant was dressed in all black, and a mask covered his face.

Her whimpering cries ignited a firestorm in his chest.

"Tunnel Creek PD! Stand down, or I will shoot! Hands in the air!"

The man made a low growl of frustration, then backed up slowly, hands raised. Suddenly, he turned and leaped at the window.

"Stop!" Jasper sprang after him.

The man dove straight into it, one arm curled over his head at impact. The earsplitting sound of breaking glass filled the room. A sickening thud, followed by the perp's strangled cry, then an ominous silence.

"Jasper, did he just…?"

"Jump out the window? Yes."

He motioned for her to stay put while he checked the room. Once he was certain there was only one assailant, he ran to the window and tugged out his flashlight. A breeze blew into the room, the scent of muggy summer air clashing with the blowing AC. He thrust the curtains aside, then peered down, using the flashlight to highlight the outcome.

Jasper pushed off the windowsill with a frustrated sigh. The man landed on the back porch roof, then fell off on the west side—directly onto the sharp head of an ornate metal fence.

There'd be no interrogating this one.

Kinsley appeared beside him, then gasped. She slapped a hand over her mouth at the gruesome sight. "He's dead?"

"Appears so." He gently grasped her shoulders to turn her away. "Don't." He led her to the bed, and she sank down onto its side. "I need to call this in. Then we have to get you into town as soon as backup arrives."

"Jasper, wait. I don't think that was the same man who attacked me at the t-tunnel."

"You're sure?"

"This person was thicker. Heavier. The man at the tunnel was slimmer. Their voices were different too."

He nodded then stepped into the hallway, sharing the details of the intruder and his death with Linda. Even as he spoke, his mind reeled. Two men? Kinsley's job was based on studying living creatures, and he trusted her observational skills were top-notch. This wasn't some random attack—they were dealing with a premeditated kidnapping and possibly attempted murder. Linda relayed that Chief McCoy was at a family function and she'd contact him immediately. But right now, Jasper needed to get Kinsley to the hospital ASAP to be checked out.

He ended the call and strode back inside to check on her. Kinsley leaned over on the edge of the bed, her brow furrowed and chest still heaving. Probably wondering the same question he was: What did she have that not one, but two men would go after her like this?

Another question struck him like an electrical shock.

Had her aunt's death been an accident, as reported? Or was foul play involved?

Outside, Dash was barking as though he knew he'd missed the action. Jasper approached Kinsley with caution, noting the marks on the soft skin of her throat. He pulled back to meet her eyes, swallowing a ball of fire in his own throat.

"He choked you?"

At her sluggish nod, he scowled. "I should've come up here with you."

"You tried to. I didn't let you. But you got here in time. I'm grateful." She panted each word. "I can't believe he jumped out the window."

"Try to forget what you saw." He peered at her. "Did he hurt you anywhere else?"

"I don't think so." She crossed her arms, a protective shield.

He inspected her neck and hairline. At least the wound from the woods had clotted, though a little more blood trickled out. When she looked up, their gazes flared together.

He moved back a few inches. "Would this be a bad time to say 'I told you so'?"

"No need to. I'm already saying it to myself." She averted her face.

He rose, checked out the window. "I should probably call an ambulance for you."

"Can I just ride with you there?"

He rubbed the back of his neck. What a night this was turning into. "We can do that."

"I should've listened to you. We shouldn't have come back here. Now there's a dead man in my parents' backyard."

Was that guilt flashing through her eyes?

He kneeled in front of her, his temples still throbbing from the action and adrenaline. "Hey, this isn't your fault. He chose to come here and go after you. Then he ignored my warning and jumped out a two-story window in the dark."

She nodded slowly, but her clouded gaze told him she was still in shock. Her petite frame shook like a broken twig in a thunderstorm. When she looked at him with those blue-gray eyes he'd once known better than his own, it felt like a gut-punch.

"Kinsley?"

"This feels too much like my parents' deaths. Those were my—"

His phone beeped with a text, cutting off her next words. He gave her an apologetic grimace, then glanced down. Officer Hammond, letting him know he was still working on the crime scene near the tunnel. He'd recovered her backpack but nothing else and said the tow truck was a few minutes out.

Jasper tucked his cell in his hand and shot Kinsley a questioning look. "You ready to head downstairs?" "I'd like to clean up a little bit before we leave. The bathroom is just down the hall."

"Yeah, but make it fast. And don't touch your clothes."

They left the bedroom and she limped for the bathroom door. He gave the room a once-over; then she entered and shut the door. He paced the hallway, checking his texts.

Linda had texted that the ME was on her way. Jasper rubbed a hand down his face. He couldn't believe they needed the medical examiner here. Again.

A few minutes later Kinsley exited the bathroom, her face more troubled than before.

He set his hand on her back, guiding her down the hall. "Let's get you outside."

They left the house the same way they'd entered. Jasper retrieved Dash from the Jeep, allowing the dog his lead to sniff around the yard but keeping him close. Jasper nudged her to sit on the breezeway steps, where they waited.

"I heard the attacker ask you something right before I entered the room. 'Come on, where is it?' Is that what he said?"

"I think so." She shivered. "He asked me for a file again. Why would he want a file from *me*? I'm a wildlife biologist, not a crime boss."

"What about an animal rights group?"

She frowned. "I can't imagine an animal rights group

would come against me here. Not like that. There've been occasions where conservationists and those in my field have butted heads with construction companies and urban development teams, but that can't be the case here. If a bat colony exists in the tunnel, it would be protected because it's located in a national forest."

The approaching sound of police sirens carried through the trees. Two officers pulled in up front, halting their conversation. One of them parked their squad car in the driveway, the other on the road. A third vehicle—a black SUV—crept up the driveway and parked beside the Jeep. He and Kinsley stood up.

"Dr. Austin." Jasper gave a two-fingered wave to the short, middle-aged woman stepping out of the third vehicle. He mouthed, "Medical examiner," at Kinsley.

"Holt." Gail Austin marched over, her large bag slung over her shoulder. "Thought you were on medical leave."

Kinsley glanced his way, her brows drawn together.

"I was." He tapped his knuckles lightly on his skull. "All better."

"I'm glad to hear that. You take care of yourself now, you hear?"

"Yes, ma'am. I'll try." He kept the bite from his tone. Gail was twenty years his senior and meant well. Still, the extra mothering rankled him.

Gail's dark eyes skipped from him to Kinsley and back before settling on the house behind them. "Looks like an eventful evening."

"Too eventful," Kinsley murmured.

"Well." The medical examiner adjusted her large bag. "I certainly didn't expect to be back to this address anytime soon."

Kinsley swayed into him. He stretched his arm, cupping her upper arm gently to keep her upright. Had she connected the dots that Dr. Austin had come here after her aunt's death?

Jasper motioned past the breezeway with his free hand. "The perp went through a second-story window. Fell on a metal fence. He's behind the house, directly outside the living room window. He, uh, he won't be going anywhere soon."

Dr. Austin nodded, adjusting her glasses, then paired up with one of the officers. The two headed for the back of the house, chatting low to each other.

The other officer, Matt Reed, jogged over. Jasper dropped his arm as the older man approached and offered scratches to Dash's ears and neck.

"Heard you two had quite the ruckus here." Matt gave Kinsley a once-over. "Ms. Miller? How are you doing?"

"I've had better nights."

Matt squeezed the back of his neck. "You just drove back into town?" He released a low whistle. "Not much of a welcoming party, is it?"

Jasper cleared his throat. "I'm taking her to the hospital. As far as the house, the kitchen was torn up when we arrived, though I'm almost positive it didn't happen today. I sent the pictures already. I need you to take a few more, check for prints."

"Got it. Take care, ma'am." Matt tipped his head, then strode across the breezeway to enter the house.

Jasper crouched to rub Dash's chest, reassuring him that he was still a good boy even if he hadn't participated in the melee upstairs. Dash snuffled over his clothes and hands once more, reliving the attack through his powerful sense of smell.

"Let's get you out of here." He rose, and they headed

for his Jeep. Jasper snapped his fingers, telling Dash to sit in the back. He settled Kinsley in the front seat, then jogged around the vehicle. Their seat belts clicked in unison as they stared at the house.

"I was going to stay at the house while I was in town."

"Those plans have changed now, unfortunately."

She sighed, the frustrated sound filling the Jeep's interior.

Clearly, she was used to an ordered life and making her own decisions and plans that she'd thought out. He felt her pain deeply. "Hey, we'll figure this out."

"I have work to do, along with getting things ready for the memorial." Her voice hitched on the last word. "Where will I stay now?"

"Like I said, we'll figure that out. You're not staying here. This house is now an active crime scene."

"I can't function with *we'll figure that out*."

"Kinsley. You've only been back in Tunnel Creek for a couple hours. You've been attacked twice in that time. I don't know how, and I don't know why, but you've got a target on your back. Until we figure out why, you cannot let your guard down. Or be alone."

Which meant he couldn't leave her side again.

# THREE

Jasper leaned his shoulder against the hospital waiting room wall. A blonde toddler cried in her mom's arms across the room, feverish and antsy, the mom's soothing words drowned out by the noise. He shifted his weight, recalling the hard nights when Gabe had been sick like that, and he and Michelle would tag team care for their son.

Those were the best moments of their rocky marriage because they'd been a team. Worked together. Hadn't bickered. They both had the same goal—get their son feeling better.

Jasper sighed. Their divorce had been painful, but Michelle's death after driving intoxicated and hitting a bridge column a few months later had been even harder on Gabe.

A nurse arrived, leading the toddler and tired mom from the waiting room. The descending silence closed in on him. He checked the time on his cell. 11:42 p.m. His brother, Noah, had met Jasper on the way to the hospital, then taken Dash back to the cabin Jasper shared with his mom and Gabe. Mom's text reassured him that Gabe was safe, fast asleep in his bunk bed. He could feel the curiosity about what had happened tonight—

and *with whom*—in his mom's message. She'd grill him about it later, no doubt.

Where was Kinsley? Last he heard, the nurse was taking her to another floor for more tests. Scans. Blood work. Stitches.

He stretched his shoulders and back. Coming to the hospital had set Kinsley off. Must be from the memories of her parents' accident. Truth was, he understood. He'd hated being here after the incident with Willard Tuttle and his own head injury. He'd despised being tethered to the IVs; seeing his mom's pale, worried features. Explaining to Gabe he'd be home as soon as he could escape. Hardest of all was the grim set of the neurologist's mouth as he delivered the second blow. *Post-traumatic amnesia.*

He shook it all away, his thoughts sidestepping over to Kinsley's parents. What had she been about to say in her old bedroom? Their accident had been a bad one—even worse because she'd been in the back seat, and she'd survived while they hadn't. Who knows what she'd seen and heard that awful night. She'd barely spoken to him afterward, and within a week she'd broken things off.

He was surprised how easily the hurt still slapped him across the face after all these years.

"Officer Holt?"

A doctor stood before him, the one who'd spoken with Kinsley during intake. "Yes, sir. How's she doing?"

"Fairly well, all things considered." The fifty-something male doctor consulted an iPad for several seconds. "Ms. Miller appears to be in excellent physical condition despite her ordeal. There's no concussion, her blood work and vitals are all within normal ranges, and the surgeon just placed fourteen stitches on the laceration on her upper forehead and hairline. You're the officer who recovered her after the attack, correct?"

Fourteen stitches? "I was off duty, but yes, I found her."

"Sounds like it was good timing you were near the tunnel tonight."

He'd had the same thought at least a dozen times. Almost like God had placed him on Whisper Mountain Road, in that spot at just that moment. "I'm glad I was, too."

The doctor stepped into Jasper's personal space, the bright hallway lights shining off his glasses and bald head. "Miller is a common name, but does she happen to be related to Henry and Lisa Miller? You know, the attorney and his wife who died in that car accident a few years ago?"

Jasper bit back a sigh. Small-town gossip mill, hard at work. At least she wasn't within earshot. "Yes, but I'd rather not discuss Ms. Miller's parents. So, no concussion?"

The older man clutched the electronic device. "That's correct."

"Good. Then I'll get her statement now."

The doctor pointed down the hall to the elevator. "She's upstairs in room 212."

Jasper gave a nod and strode out of the waiting room to the elevator bank.

One minute later, he paused in the doorway of room 212. Kinsley lay in the bed, eyes closed—a small lump under the long white sheet. Her pale face had been cleaned of the dried blood and dirt from the woods, her hair falling in damp waves on the pillow.

He stepped quietly into the room, and her eyelids fluttered open.

"Jasper." Her soft smile was a surprise and completely disarming. "They gave me some drugs that make me happy."

His lips tipped up despite himself. This should be interesting. "That happens in hospitals sometimes."

"One minute I feel like skipping down the hall, and the next I want to sleep until Christmas."

"That's easy. Option two." He strode in and settled in the chair beside her. "A full night's rest is highly underappreciated."

"I appreciate it." She yawned as if on cue, then peered at him. "You look like an adult now, Jasper. A real adult."

He rubbed the back of his neck. Composed and serious Kinsley had been set free. "As opposed to a fake one?"

"No, I think you're real."

"I am turning thirty next month."

"Me too."

That's right. Her birthday was a week after his, in July. Every year, she came to mind on that day. He'd prayed for her. Prayed she was well. Happy. Prayed away the bitterness.

He fisted his cell, retrieved the notepad from his pocket and tapped the pen to the four-by-six cover. Time to get down to business. "I'm sorry you'll have to go over this again, but I need all the details you can remember for your statement."

"Does your son look like you?"

Where had that come from? "You'll meet him eventually. I don't think so. But I am told he acts like me."

"Oh. Well, I'm not sure that's a good thing. You're very stubborn."

Was she teasing him? Jasper tucked away another

smile. Kinsley must be a lightweight with pain medication. "You sure you're up for this right now?"

She waved her fingers in a *no big deal* gesture. "I want to get it over with."

"Okay. Here we go." He reclined in the seat, then activated the voice recorder on his cell. "Ms. Miller, please tell me what exactly happened at Whisper Mountain Tunnel this evening, the sixteenth day of June…"

Kinsley recounted the first part of the evening in rambling sentences. She jumped from the reason she was at the tunnel to the moments before the first assailant came after her. He jotted down a note to call her supervisor and the coworker who'd tipped her off at the zoo. She shared that she was conducting a study on bat feeding patterns and knew the area well, so it had presented a perfect opportunity to observe them in the wild.

Unfortunately, coming home had also placed her in a dangerous situation.

His chest tightened. He clicked the pen, then clicked it again. "So why were you there alone tonight? You could've called me. I would've come along."

"Didn't we discuss this earlier?" She frowned. "I prefer being by myself for observation. Most people are too noisy—" she gave him and his pen a pointed look "—and scare the animals off."

"An attractive woman, alone in the woods at night." Maybe not the best choice of words but the truth, nonetheless. He kept clicking. "No weapon for self-defense."

She sat up a little straighter. "I believe you and your pen are judging me."

"No," he said, stretching out the denial, clicking even faster. "Just trying to get answers."

*"Jasper."*

He flicked his thumb off the end of the pen. Rolled it across his palm until the unaccounted-for anger dissipated.

"I'm a wildlife biologist." She clutched the bedsheet, her earlier goodwill toward him gone. "I go into the field at least twice a month. It's part of my job. By *field*, I mean woods, forest, swamp—whatever is called for. Usually alone. I do carry a utility knife."

"To slit your attacker's bootlaces?"

Her eyes narrowed. "I've spent my entire adult life on my own—and up until this point, I've been just fine, thank you very much. I lived and worked in a big city for years and this has never happened."

"Okay. I'm sorry. I'll drop it. Now, moving on." He clicked the pen as quietly as he could in order to continue writing. "Is there anyone at your work you've upset? A former coworker, a..." He cleared his throat. "An ex-boyfriend?"

"No." She dropped the sheet and stared at her nails. "I don't think so. I haven't really...dated much, and I get along with my coworkers. I mean, we're there because of our love of animals, you know? That bonds us together."

"What about here? Could there be anyone in Tunnel Creek you might've upset? An enemy from high school?"

"I don't think so." Her face fell. "At least, I hope not."

She seemed so alone, like an island of a person, that he touched her arm for a brief moment. "You and your family were well-liked, from all accounts."

"Thank you."

His cell beeped. "Hold on." He opened the screen, blinking rapidly at what he was reading. Things were getting more complicated by the moment. He set the phone on his thigh. "About this file. Do you have any idea what these men are referring to? Paperwork you would be carrying from your work or the zoo?"

"I don't have a file, other than for the species I'm studying. Myotis grisescens."

"Say what?"

"The gray bat." She blinked patiently at him. "For this trip, I also brought info about Sumter National Forest, plus my biologist ID in case a park ranger needed to see it, but that was all."

Jasper finished writing, then looked up. The medicinal haze had disappeared from her eyes, leaving behind a fear-filled expression.

"Can't the police—I mean, you—look up who that man was at my parents' house and find something out?"

"Done. Steven Ames, forty-one. Has—*had*—a three-page rap sheet and four prior arrests occurring all over the southeast. Petty theft, burglary."

"And he—both of the men—knew *my* name." She tucked her lips between her teeth. "We can't argue with the evidence, then."

"Which is…?"

"That there's nothing random about this."

"Uh, no." He set the notepad down and stood, pacing the room. When he turned, her features were twisted with distress. He hated to make it worse, but she needed to know.

"Here's the thing, Kinsley. I was just notified that the man in your parents' house is from Atlanta. The address for his apartment is five minutes from your place."

Kinsley gathered her hair into a loose bun, flinching when she tugged too hard. She gazed at the lopsided result and her tired reflection in the hospital bathroom's mirror. A bandage hid the sore, sutured wound along her hairline. She pressed her fingertips to the soft, spiky patch they'd shaved to reach the rest of the wound.

Twenty-four hours ago, she'd been packing for her trip to Tunnel Creek. Wiping away tears. Dealing with dread about the empty house she'd face. Now she sat in a hospital room with a head wound, wracking her tired brain about what this file was her attackers had referred to.

Jasper's warning rang in her ears again: *The man in your parents' house is from Atlanta. The address for his apartment is five minutes from your place.*

But why? The pain medication was wearing off, leaving behind a dull headache and a chilling sense that there was nowhere to hide in this town *or* back at her apartment.

She shivered and gave her reflection a last once-over. At least her side bangs covered the shaved part, and she no longer had to wear the itchy, gaping gown.

She opened the bathroom door and shuffled over to the chair beside the bed. Her crumpled backpack sat on the floor in front of the chair. An officer had brought it in earlier and given it to Jasper, minus all her equipment.

Kinsley rubbed her eyes. What if she didn't get the items back?

"It's the least of my worries."

She looked around the room. Jasper had stepped outside to make calls for the investigation. And give her a few minutes of privacy. He'd known she needed that without her even saying it, which was thoughtful of him. She dropped into the chair he had occupied. The warmth from his body remained on the cushions, the smell of soap and cedar still lingering.

Soft footsteps sounded from the hallway, and a shadow fell under the door. It hovered there, unmoving. Her spine stiffened, and her breath hiccupped. Had someone just knocked, or was that her pulse thudding in her ears?

The door handle turned, opened an inch. *Creak.* Two inches. Her heart climbed into her throat, and she rose from the chair on shaky limbs. Another doctor? No, she'd just been checked. The person outside the room had a furtive way about them that raised the fine hairs on her arms. *Creak.* The door opened wider, and the tip of a silver knife flashed under the fluorescent lighting. Kinsley's legs gave out, and she crashed backward onto the bed.

She scrambled upright. Two nurses' voices carried down the hall, and the door slapped shut. Quick footsteps followed. The shadow disappeared in the opposite direction of the women and the nurses' station.

She crossed the room, her chest heaving. Was there a way to lock the door? She glanced toward her cell, which was lying on the cabinet against the wall. She should call Jasper.

Someone knocked on the door, and she jumped, grabbing a clipboard. Held it up like a weapon. "Who is it?"

"Kinsley?" Jasper's face appeared through the cracked-open door. "Just me." He stepped inside. "What is it? Did something happen?"

She set the clipboard down with a clatter. "Someone was out there…in the hall. They had a knife! Then the nurses walked down this way, and the person disappeared."

"Which way?"

She pointed to her right.

"Toward the stairwell." He buzzed the intercom, asking a nurse to come down the hall. "Once the nurse gets here, I'll take a look in the stairwell. But I'm not leaving you alone again."

He moved closer to the window and made a quick call. Kinsley collapsed into the chair as he relayed the information to another officer apparently stationed at the front of the hospital.

A nurse entered. "Ms. Miller, how are you feeling? Did you need more pain medication?"

"I'm the one who called." Jasper hung up and treaded over. "Can you stay with her while I check the stairwell? Two minutes?"

The nurse patted her brown hair. "Sure. Is something wrong?"

"Maybe. I'll be right back." He disappeared, and Kinsley's gaze transferred from Jasper's retreating back to the squatly built nurse.

"Did you happen to see anyone near my room a couple minutes ago?"

The nurse—Sharie, her name badge stated—tilted her head. "No, hon. I was busy, though. Oh, wait. There was a dad here. He visited the young lady two doors down. It's his daughter. She broke her arm falling off her bike. I can go ask him if he came to the wrong room."

"No, don't interrupt them. Thank you, though." It couldn't be him.

Jasper reentered the room, his features set in stone. He dismissed Sharie with a thank-you wave, then addressed Kinsley, his chest rising and falling. "Stairwell was empty. The guard at the front desk didn't see anything out of the ordinary."

She felt like she couldn't catch her breath. "Why is this happening?"

"We don't know. I'm sorry." He set a palm on her shoulder briefly. "What I do know is, it's not safe for you to be without protection. Because of that, you're coming with me tonight."

"What?" Kinsley drew back, taking a lap across the hospital room. Her thoughts scattered when Jasper stood in such close proximity. "I can get a hotel room. Wouldn't that be safe?"

"Not safe enough."

"Jasper, I refuse to put your family in danger."

"We won't be." He approached her slowly, as though she was a wild animal about to flee. "You're a smart woman, Kinsley. Think about it. Being by yourself is not an option right now."

She couldn't deny the reality of his statement. The knife's serrated blade had cut into her psyche. "But it's your home."

"We had new windows and a top-notch security system installed in the cabin last year. Plus, my brother Noah comes and goes. Trust me, it's safe there. And it shouldn't be for long. Two, three days, tops."

"Thank you, but I'd rather not be an imposition in any of your lives." She clutched her arms across her chest.

"Who's being stubborn now?"

She glared at him.

"There's a bedroom on the second floor with a private bathroom. Mom would love the female company."

A question lingered that she couldn't ignore. Speaking it aloud pinched her pride.

"What about…us? Do you think she'd mind me staying with you and your family after…?" *After all that happened between us?*

"You're a citizen in danger in my town, and it's the

best option while we investigate the case. Anyway, my mom's favorite expression is *grow in grace*."

Kinsley had attended church during her childhood and young adult years. She remembered enough to know that *growing in grace* meant showing others' kindness even if they didn't deserve it. Like Jesus had.

"So, she doesn't hold grudges."

"No, she doesn't."

"Okay." She tucked her shoulders, noting that Jasper hadn't said *he* didn't hold any grudges. "I'll do it. But only one night."

Kinsley side-eyed Jasper as he answered his buzzing phone. He was an honorable man whose duty was to serve and protect, even someone who'd once hurt him. She was grateful that he was here for her in this desperate time of need. Her chest warmed. Maybe once this was all over, they'd part ways on much better terms than the last time.

"There's been another development."

The chill in his rumbling voice jerked her chin up.

"I sent a local deputy sheriff to check your apartment. Just heard back. It's torn up. Window busted in the bedroom. Your desk drawers were emptied all over the floor."

Kinsley reached for the chair and sank into it. She felt like a robin hatchling in its nest with a hungry crow circling overhead. Her apartment too?

He continued, "Someone must've gone through it as soon as you left—"

"And didn't find what they were looking for. So they followed me."

"Very possible." Jasper crossed his arms. "Whatever they're looking for—'they' being the criminals who attacked you—they believe you still have it. Which reinforces that you need protection until we figure out what they want."

Kinsley pulled her legs to her chest to stop the quivering in her stomach. What would've happened if she'd been at her apartment—alone—when one of the men broke in? Goose bumps shimmied over her arms. They needed to find out what these men wanted, or else...

Or else she might not live through the next attack.

# FOUR

Jasper navigated his unmarked Charger up the winding driveway. The rising sun broke over his place atop the mountain, shooting yellow sunbursts in every direction. But he was too weary to appreciate the beauty this morning. His muscles felt like Gabe's Silly Putty after it'd been squeezed through his son's fingers for an hour. He and Kinsley had been at the hospital almost all night. Now he was taking her home.

To *his* home.

He shook off the odd feeling that thought brought then glanced at Kinsley, who was huddled in the passenger seat. She'd been quiet the entire ride, and he'd been preoccupied doing mental gymnastics about the case. Before they left the hospital, Jasper had studied the lobby and parking lot. Asked the nurses again. Reviewed security footage and found the cameras on Kinsley's floor and the adjacent stairwell had shorted out.

Of course. *Shorted out* being police speak for "tampered with."

Jasper ground his teeth and wished his steering wheel was his gym's punching bag, but it wouldn't help to get angry.

He tucked the car into his usual parking spot, between the two-story cabin and the smaller original cabin, now

his mom's art studio. Kinsley had no idea why someone would be after her or what information they'd want.
Which made these assaults and this case even more up-
setting. If he couldn't figure out the *what*, how could he
pinpoint the *why*?

Officer Hammond had run background checks on the
deceased attacker and found no connections to Kinsley.
All the man's priors had occurred throughout Georgia
and South Carolina. Atlanta. Greenville. Columbia. Steven Ames had no relatives in Tunnel Creek. So why had
he come after her?

Jasper had placed a call into her work, asking the
zoo's general manager to get back to him. So far, no call-
backs. There must be something there—or someone—
who would help connect all these dots.

Movement erupted from the front of the cabin. He
craned his neck. *Gabe?* Instead, his mom pushed open
the screen door, releasing their four-legged welcoming
committee. The dogs thundered down the front porch.

"You have a pack." Kinsley gaped as the trio of ca-
nines surrounded the vehicle. "That's quite a security
system."

"Plus, Dash. He's around here somewhere."

"Are those two redbone coonhounds?"

Of course she knew dog breeds. "Yes. Brothers, Leo
and Mike. Named after Leonardo and Michelangelo."

"The cartoon turtles or the artists?"

He chuckled. Kinsley joking around was a treat.
"The artists."

"Like your mom?"

His brows shot up. She remembered his mom was an
artist. "That's right. She rescued Leo and Mike at four
months, after their owner was hurt in a hunting accident
and couldn't care for them. Renamed them, of course.
The German shepherd is Trek. He's a retired deputy."

"He's very handsome. Are they okay with strangers?"

"Leo and Mike are only dangerous to raccoons and possums. They're pretty friendly. Trek is the guard dog, but you're with me, so you're good."

She pressed her hand to the window as Leo jumped up on the passenger side, his pink-and-black jowls leaving slobber marks on the glass.

"Leo! Get down. Man. I just had this washed."

"Is this why you think I'm safer here?"

"A big part of the reason, yes."

She stilled beside him. "I've been thinking, Jasper."

"Don't do too much of that."

She snorted softly. "Yes, well. I realized that I never said goodbye to your mom. She was so nice to me, welcoming. She even…" She glanced his way. "She sent me a condolence card and flowers for my parents' service. I'm horrified to admit I don't recall saying thank you."

"You were seventeen, Kinsley. It's okay. I told you, she doesn't hold grudges."

"You don't seem to, either." She stared at her lap.

"Oh, I'm furious." He pasted on a grin when she looked his way. *Deflecting*, or whatever the head doctors called it. Because the truth was, what had happened between them—what she had done—still stung. "My mom will probably smother you with hugs or bread or coffee. Or cheese sculptures."

"Don't apologize for bread or coffee, ever. And what on earth is a cheese sculpture?"

"You'll have to ask her. I just eat them."

A child's voice interrupted them then, followed by a flurry of motion in his peripheral vision. Gabriel. His chest warmed. When had his little boy started looking like such a big kid?

"Daddy! Dad, Dad. I caught a sal-mander. Look, look! It's black and blue."

He stepped out of the Charger. Kinsley exited on her side, scratching ears and fur and cooing to the dogs. His mom whistled for them to come back inside. Kinsley circled the back of the vehicle, joining him as his fair-haired six-year-old bounded up the hill beside the driveway. His small hands cradled something. Dash shadowed Gabe, ever watchful and protective.

"Look, look! Can I keep it?" Gabe raced over, bumping into Jasper's leg. He wore a proud smile. "Its name is Lizzy, for *lizard.* Look at her blue tail. Who's that? Did you 'rest her?"

Jasper eyed the slimy critter in his son's palms but kept his distance. "Hello, Lizzy. Whoa, that's quite a tail there. Definitely blue." He glanced at Kinsley. "Ms. Kinsley wasn't arrested. She's…an old friend who's staying for a couple days."

"Hi. She doesn't look old. Why's she hurt like that?"

Kinsley waved. "Hi, Gabe."

Jasper ruffled Gabe's hair. "She's not old. I've known her a long time. She got busted up last night. That's why I wasn't here to eat breakfast with you this morning."

"Gwama made blueberry pancakes."

"Aw, man," Jasper pretended to sob. "I missed those?" He ran his knuckles down his cheeks like he was mopping up tears. "Did you save me any?"

"No."

"What?"

"I ate four. Uncle Noah ate *seven.*"

Jasper made oinking sounds. "You're going to be eating more than me and Noah soon."

Kinsley inched forward, palms out. "Can I see the lizard? I love lizards."

Gabe's sand-colored eyes popped wide. "*You* wanna hold Lizzy?"

"Sure. I won't hurt her. Or him. It looks like a blue-tailed skink."

"Yeah, a stink. It's a girl one."

Jasper chuckled and stepped away, heading for the porch. His son wouldn't leave Kinsley alone now that he knew she also liked wiggly creatures that hid under rocks. A strange sense of pride stretched his heart. Despite her parents' deaths, despite being on her own in the world, she'd followed her dreams. Become a wildlife biologist, like she'd always talked about in high school.

He leaped up the steps and offered his mom a fist bump, followed by a quick peck on her shoulder-length, silver-streaked dark hair. She wore her usual faded jean shorts, paint-splattered T-shirt and an untied *Starry Night* paint smock.

"You all right?" Mom pressed her arm into his, bracelets jangling. She was only a few inches shorter than him. He'd gotten his height from her—not to mention his stubbornness.

"Tired. Long night."

"How is your head?"

He tapped a fingertip to the top of his noggin. "Still attached."

"Jasper. You're supposed to be taking it easy. Do you have to go back to the station today?"

"Yep. Chief needs the reports. Kinsley can rest here for a while, then she has to come in."

"Poor thing. What a terrible *welcome home* this was."

"I don't think she considers this home anymore. She came back for Rhonda's memorial, wasn't planning on staying long from what I could tell."

Mom's drawn-out *hmm* tweaked his tired nerves. Because he knew where her wild imagination would lead next.

"It's a shame. You two were such a cute couple."

"Mom—" he held a palm out like he was stopping traffic "—*cute* is for puppies. There is no way I'd trust her again. Especially with a little boy who'd grow as attached as moss on rocks, then have his heart broken. Not happening. I've learned my lesson the hard way. Twice. First Kinsley, then M—"

He cut his wife's name off with a shake of his head. *Michelle.* She'd despised Tunnel Creek more than she loved him. Or their son.

"Jasper David. Don't compare Michelle and Kinsley. That young woman out there lost both her parents as a teenager, while Michelle was a grown woman who knew her own mind. Their situations are different."

"Fine, but none of it matters anyway. Kinsley and I had our moment, and we crashed and burned. She's a scientist studying bats now, thinks there's some out at the tunnel."

"Bats? Huh. Well, it looks like she enjoys all of God's creatures. And little boys."

They watched as Kinsley and Gabe parked themselves side by side on the large rock edging the steeper part of the driveway, passing the lizard between them. When the creature scuttered up Gabe's T-shirt sleeve, they both laughed like it was adorable.

He shuddered. "Great. Gabe'll be asking her to stay here forever by lunchtime."

Mom's dark brown eyes, so much like his own, met his. Sympathetic affection shone from them. "Do you have any leads for her case?"

He rammed a hand through his hair, hating the answer he had to give. "Not really." He relayed what had occurred so far, ending with the hospital situation. "Seeing how she's been attacked and threatened three times already, you'd think she'd know why they're after her."

"*Three* times?"

"Unfortunately, yes." He cracked his back, then yawned. "Kinsley is an intelligent, levelheaded woman with good instincts. She saw someone about to come into her hospital room with a knife, and I believe her."

*Speaking of...* Kinsley strolled over, Gabe glued to her side. His face beamed with happiness. And he was empty-handed? How'd she convinced him to let the lizard go?

They mounted the bottom step. "Gabe and I decided Lizzy should go back to the rocks and trees, with her family."

"I'm much appreciative of that," Jasper teased, avoiding eye contact with their guest.

"Miss Kinshley said we can catch a cricket later and bring it to Lizzy's home for her dinner." Gabe danced from one foot to the other like it was the greatest idea in the world.

*"Kinsley,"* Jasper corrected gently. He clicked his tongue at Trek, who had begged back outside, descended the stairs and shoved his back against Kinsley's side, asking for scratches.

"Thank you for letting me stay here, Mrs. Holt." She stroked the shepherd's neck.

His mom leaned in, wrapping Kinsley in a hug. "Of course. I'm sorry for your loss. Rhonda was such a thoughtful woman. We volunteered at the new hospice home in town together several times. Years ago, she bought two of my paintings from an art show. Really helped me out, and I've never forgotten that. She was a gem." Mom released Kinsley from the hug. "And please call me Dana."

"Thank you." Kinsley's brow furrowed. "I think she hung one painting in my dad's office and the other in her bedroom. I'll make sure I get those before the house is sold."

"Oh, well, you do with them what you think is best."

"I'd like to keep them."

His mom offered a bittersweet smile. "I'm glad you're back in Tunnel Creek. Though I wish—" she glanced at Jasper "—it was under different circumstances."

"I just don't want to be an inconvenience."

"You are not an inconvenience. You're welcome here." She spread her hands out to stress her point. Her multicolored nails stood out in the sunshine. "This is the safest place you could be."

"That's what Jasper said, too." Kinsley glanced his way.

Jasper scratched the stubble on his chin. Enough with the touchy-feely reunion. "Let's get you inside. Get you some food. I'm starving."

"I have sandwich meat and rolls," his mom called out from behind them. "She can shower and rest, whatever she needs to do. Oh, there's a cheddar duck if you want that. I have crackers!"

"Let me guess," Kinsley murmured as they climbed the staircase. "The cheese sculptures."

"Yep. The Gouda one melted last week, and she tried Swiss… Not so good. Too holey."

Their gazes collided at the top of the stairs, humor sparking between them like an electrical cord. They grinned at each other.

"Your mom is so fun." Her eyes crinkled, light flaring inside them.

"Yeah, she's something else. Come on." He continued down the hall to the spare room.

"Here it is." After setting the suitcase down in front of the closet doors, he ambled over to the lone window. It opened up to the wild green hills folding into Sumter National Forest.

She joined him at the window. "I forgot how beautiful it is here."

"Sounds like that was for the best."

She swallowed, and he watched the motion of her pale, delicate throat. A throat that had been squeezed painfully hours ago. He drew in a measured breath.

"I'm sorry you came back to this. Though I have a feeling you're safer here than alone in Atlanta."

"I don't know if I'll ever feel safe again." A forlorn expression hijacked her lovely features. He checked the window locks and closed the blinds. His thoughts drifted to Willard Tuttle's murder. Could there be a tie between the two cases? Seemed unlikely. Someone was clearly after incriminating information they believed Kinsley had. His guess was it had to do with her work. They wanted her gone from the zoo she worked in. Wanted her position. Something.

"Would there be important information or files you keep in your office at the zoo or at home that someone would want?" He'd put in a call to have a local deputy take a look at her work office.

"I considered that after you told me about the break-in at my apartment. But there's nothing. Scientific articles, maps of the region, photographs of animals, papers from field studies—nothing important enough to cause *this*." She motioned wildly at her head wound. "Do you think these men will try to kill me if I don't figure out where and what this file is?"

Their eyes met. Sunlight snuck in through the cracked blinds, highlighting her injured face and strawberry blonde hair, the thick bandage on the side of her forehead.

"Someone is after you, and they want something from you bad enough to send at least two men." He jammed his hands into his pockets. "Yes, I think that's a possibility. And for that reason, you cannot be alone."

Kinsley stood at the top of the cabin stairs and squared her shoulders. She almost felt like herself again. A battered, sore version, at least. She wasn't supposed to get her hair or face soaked, so she'd cleaned up in the bathroom, then flip-flopped on the guest bed like a trout on a riverbank. For two hours she'd tried to sleep, but all she ended up doing was reliving the attacks, the horrible feel of the men's rough hands on her skin.

And wondering what file they were referring to.

A dull ache spread out from the head wound, emphasized by certain actions and facial expressions. She descended the staircase quietly but froze at the bottom step. Jasper and Dana Holt murmured to each other nearby. In the kitchen?

"Eat something, please," Dana pleaded.

Definitely the kitchen.

"Don't have much of an appetite." Jasper's voice was gruff. Even without seeing him, Kinsley could picture his creased brow and the way his mouth folded in on one side when he was deep in thought or stressed. Like last night at the hospital.

*Because of her.*

She slumped forward. Her situation had driven a wedge into Jasper's orderly life, and she hated how that bled into his family. *Bled.* Kinsley touched her bandage, cringing.

A chair pushed back from the table, and she hurried off the last step. Everything swayed at her sudden movement, and her hand shot out for solid ground. Jasper appeared in the hallway. He took in her shaky movements, her death grip on the handrail, and rushed forward.

"Hey, careful. What're you doing up?"

"Falling back down, apparently."

He offered his arm, and they proceeded down the hallway like a newly married couple would out of a church. Just the way they'd talked and dreamed about their senior year. She mashed her lips together at the unexpected observation.

"Did you sleep at all?" he asked.

"I *rested*. There's so much going on I just couldn't."

"I get it. Same."

They entered the kitchen, and she leaned forward to catch Dana's eye. "Thank you for having me here. The guest bed is really comfortable."

"Anytime, Kinsley. Really."

Kinsley blinked into the golden afternoon sun, which entered the room through the wide window over the sink. "Where's Gabe?"

"Getting dirty." Jasper cracked open the fridge, offering her a fruit drink. She accepted it with a murmured *thank you*.

"He's digging for worms out back," Dana explained. "He got some watermelon seeds, and he'll be planting those in the garden with me later."

"Sounds like you have a little farmer on your hands."

Jasper shut the refrigerator, then uncapped an iced tea. "If it involves dirt or critters, he's there."

"There's nothing wrong with that."

"Guess not. It worked okay for you." He swiped a napkin across his mouth. "You up for going into the station, checking some mug shots? Chief McCoy would like to talk with you."

The police chief? Kinsley choked on a gulp of juice. "Um, s-sure."

Ten minutes later they loaded into Jasper's work car. On the way out, he caught Gabe watering the bucketful of worm-filled dirt in the side yard. Kinsley had stepped in, saved the night crawlers from their watery grave and explained how to care for them. Jasper had kissed Gabe's dripping hair, then they'd left, the boy calling out *goodbyes* for thirty seconds.

"Thanks for taking care of those for me."

Kinsley smiled at his exaggerated way of saying *those* about the night crawlers. "I don't mind. He's a sweetheart."

Jasper clicked on the AC. "Except at bedtime."

"It's a childhood requirement to refuse to sleep at night, isn't it?"

He chuckled. "I guess it is. I'm just grateful my mom's around to help. Parenting is tiring."

"His mom... Does he remember her?"

"Bits and pieces. Only the good stuff, thank the Lord. I mean, I think God made us that way, you know?"

Goose bumps prickled her skin from the air-conditioning and his words. "'That way,' as in how we're able to still see the sunset even as the rest of the world is going dark?"

He glanced at her as they passed the mailbox. "Right. The *cup half full* kind of deal. Kids ace that. We adults, not so much."

"Grief changes people, that's for certain." She paused. "I'm sorry for his loss. And yours."

"Thank you."

After checking for oncoming traffic, he turned onto the road that headed into town. She gazed out the window, soaking in the quiet as the world exploded in vivid shades of green. Sumter National Park was stunning in the summer, the heat often tapering off to a cool evening perfect for stargazing and time on the back porch.

Just like she used to do with her parents. She closed her eyes, fighting off memories more bitter than sweet.

His voice broke her reverie. "How's the wound?"

"It still stings a bit. I took a pain reliever before I lay

down." She traced the reapplied bandage with a finger, a question taking root. "What did your mom mean earlier when she asked about your head? And the medical examiner? She said something about it, too."

He didn't answer, instead frowning into the rearview mirror like he'd done when he first found her last night. Then he adjusted his grip on the wheel, his face a mask of concentration.

"Jasper, what's wrong?"

"Looks like someone's in a hurry," Jasper murmured. "Come on."

Kinsley twisted in the seat. A dark blue older-model truck closed in on them, spitting gravel. Weaving back and forth.

She faced forward, her heart knocking into her ribs. "Do they want to pass?"

"I don't—hold on! He's trying to hit us!" Jasper jabbed at a button on his dash. The crackle of radio static prickled her ears.

"Look out!" Kinsley screamed, pointing in front of them.

Another vehicle—a white minivan—drove directly in front of them from the opposite direction. And they were stuck right smack in the middle.

# FIVE

Jasper's elbows locked as he steered toward the second vehicle. His choices were limited, and his chest heaved as he continued forward. *God, protect us. Let this work.*

The minivan was fifty yards away. Then forty. Had the drivers ambushed them here on purpose? Trees hugged the roadside, cutting off any chance of fleeing. The big truck rode his bumper like a flea on a dog.

Fifteen yards.

"Brace yourself!" Jasper jerked the wheel hard right, placing himself in the line of danger if they collided. But the van turned hard to its right as well. Wheels spun. Stones and dirt pinged the Charger's windows. Jasper's muscles cranked as he fought the momentum of the spin. Inches separated the two vehicles. Kinsley's scream seared his eardrums as they spun onto the narrow shoulder, smashing wildflowers and low-lying bushes and everything in their path.

A *pop, pop, pop* sent jolts of adrenaline through his veins.

The van was a decoy so the truck driver could get shots in.

"Get down!" He threw an arm over Kinsley's huddled form, steering them off the shoulder and back onto the road. Pressed the gas and dragged in a ragged breath. The van was far behind them now. Only the large blue truck gave chase. He accelerated until they were traveling nearly twice the legal speed limit.

Kinsley peeked up. "Where are we going?"

"Away. Stay down." Jasper was pretty sure whoever was chasing them was shooting at the tires, which meant they were trying to disable the vehicle to get to Kinsley again. *Why?*

An idea formed. He hated to execute it while Kinsley was with him, but right now there was no choice. He wanted answers about her attackers, and this was the way to get them.

Two more bullets struck the car. One hit the back window with a crackling *pop*. Maybe they weren't just shooting at tires.

She dove to the floorboard. "Jasper! Be careful!"

"I'm trying." Sweat breached his brow, stinging his eyes. He rubbed them and narrowed his gaze. Another couple hundred feet...

There! A hidden road he knew well. At the last minute, Jasper turned left. As soon as the Charger was straight, he hit the gas again. The big truck—a Dodge, from what he could tell—turned, too. But the driver didn't stop. He tailed him from a ways back, the headlights dogging them for each twist and turn in the private road.

Thank the Lord for extra horsepower. The road rose up a hill, then snaked down into a low, long valley. A lake sparkled in the center, edged on one side by an old two-story wood-and-stone building. Attached to the building was a massive water wheel. Behind him, the truck dropped out of sight.

She peeked up again. "Is this the grist mill?"

"Yep." He and Gabe hiked this property on his days off. The dogs swam in the lake in summer. "We're hitting a dead end here in about fifteen seconds. Stay down."

"Can you see him?"

"Not right now. He slowed down before the hill."

"Maybe he stopped. Turned around."

Not likely. Which was part of the plan. "I'm going to lure him in, and he won't have anywhere to go."

"Can you call someone? Or call this in?"

"Already did." The Radio Distress button on his dash had sent a message to dispatch to let them know there was trouble, along with his location.

Still no sign of the truck. *Had* he turned around? Doubtful. Jasper cut through the grassy field that served as a parking lot when the mill was open. He fit the Charger behind the small square building that sat in front of the mill, the ticket booth for visitors of the historic site. Thank the Lord it was closed for visitors today. The shrubs surrounding the ticket booth were tall and almost overgrown. Hopefully, they'd camouflage his car.

He put it in Park.

"Why did you lead him here?" She stared behind them.

"Ambush."

"Yeah, *us*! We're sitting ducks."

"Quack."

She turned to face him. "*Jasper.* Why're you joking about this?"

"I'm not. Just trust me. We'll keep him busy for the next five minutes, until backup arrives."

"Like another police officer?"

"Exactly like that." Jasper exited the vehicle, then

jogged to her side of the car. Still no sign of the truck. *Huh.* Maybe the driver had given up.

"So what are we doing?"

"Cornering him like he thinks he's cornering us." He helped her out, canvassing the road leading to the mill. "Remember coming here for youth group on the Fourth of July?"

"Yes, but we weren't being chased by a man with a gun."

"I've got one, too." He patted his huge black tool belt. "Come on."

They sprinted to the side of the rambling historic grist mill. He jangled the lock, then pushed on the door that led into the basement-level floor. It groaned like it didn't want to reveal its secrets.

"Jasper...?"

He shoved the bottom of the door with his boot, then pressed on the middle. It shuddered, then creaked open. He shut it behind them and plunged deeper into the belly of the building, keeping her close. The inside of the mill smelled of damp earth, decaying wood and something rotting. He cringed. Fifteen steps in, Kinsley froze beside him. She sank to her knees.

"What are you doing?"

"Look at this." She motioned at something on the floor, then looked up.

Her tone almost sounded...happy?

"What? We have to move." He slipped out his cell and tapped the light, leaning down. "What is that?"

She pointed at something on the ground again. "It's guano. Bat droppings."

He grimaced. "We don't have time right now—"

"There might be gray bats in here." Her voice rose with excitement. *Only Kinsley.*

The rumble of a vehicle engine crashed into the stone walls surrounding them.

"That's got to be him. Move!"

Jasper directed her deeper into the basement. *Bat droppings*. The woman was way too focused on critters. The ground became uneven. Cobwebs sagged across the log ceiling like tiny speed traps. One caught on the top of his head. He swatted it away. She probably liked those nasty little creatures, too.

Faint light infiltrated the darkness.

"What're those?" She pointed to a long wall covered with containers.

"Grain bins." A shadowy corner caught his eye. "There they are."

"What?"

"Stairs. We're going to the mill's first floor." They mounted the narrow staircase, the soft wood complaining with each rushed step. A loud creak carried up to them. The door. Their pursuer was inside.

Jasper's heart thrashed. "He's inside. Hurry."

"How do you know," she panted at the top, "that it's not your backup?"

"The officer would identify himself."

They burst through the door on the first floor. The staircase emptied out into a hallway. Sunlight spilled through a windowed door to their left; and to the right, the hall turned a corner toward the main entrance. He motioned her to the door.

"Where are we going now?" She slowed at the exit. The upper half of the door was glass. He moved her aside then shoved his elbow into it, shattering the surface into a dozen pieces. Kinsley gaped at him as he pushed the broken pieces out then carefully wiggled the large remaining shard.

"Jasper…?"

"Just in case." He fisted the glass. "Can't shoot him. I need info."

She gave a wobbly nod, and they rushed outside.

"Watch your step. I want you to go over there." A four-foot-high wood booth sat on the side, *Cotton Candy and Drinks* painted in large letters on its front. She scurried behind it. "Stay there while I wait for him."

A siren wailed in the distance. *Finally.*

Footsteps pounded down the hallway. The man had found the staircase, too. Jasper pressed up beside the door. Across the deck, the enormous water wheel spun, spitting out water like it had done for a couple hundred years. As though everything was normal and there weren't men with guns about to come to blows.

Jasper tensed as the steps approached. The black-clad assailant busted through the door, sending it against the wall opposite Jasper. He leaped toward their pursuer, grabbing one arm and reaching for the other. The man ducked and spun away, the glint of a gun catching Jasper's eye. In his peripheral, a blond head appeared. The attacker turned, aiming for the booth and Kinsley.

"Stay down!" Jasper dove for cover behind a stack of chairs as gunfire exploded, bullets pinging into the front of the wooden booth.

Jasper rolled to a crouch. He only had a second. With a flick of his wrist, he sent the glass flying at the man's leg.

A hit!

The man's howl punctuated the air as he bent in half, clutching his lower-right leg. Jasper lunged forward, straight for the gun hand to disarm him.

The attacker fell to the deck, a colorful string of curse

words proclaiming how he felt about Jasper's tactics. Crimson pooled below his leg.

Jasper smacked the gun away, then stretched the man's arms behind his back. He withdrew his handcuffs and slapped them on. "You chased the wrong guy. You're under arrest."

"Nah... Don't want you... Was after *her.*"

"You're not touching her."

The man grumbled under his breath, then he sagged onto the wood. Passed out.

Jasper met Kinsley's wide eyes across the deck. "Hey, it's okay. Just wait there until the other officer gets up here."

She swayed into the booth. "He's the...person who attacked me near the tunnel. I recognize his voice."

Her terrified gaze clung to the incapacitated man as Jasper checked the assailant's pulse. From what he could tell, the glass had hit its mark and then fell. It wasn't imbedded. The wound would likely be superficial, and the criminal would still be able to undergo questioning once it was sewn up.

One suspect was dead, the other in custody. Lord willing, they'd get some answers now about why they were targeting Kinsley.

Kinsley wilted in the chair inside Chief McCoy's office at the Tunnel Creek Police Department. The air-conditioning blew directly on her, turning her body to ice.

"This is quite a situation, Ms. Miller." Chief McCoy appeared to be in his late fifties, his silver hair and thick mustache perfectly groomed. His steel gray eyes took note of her hand-wringing and shivering limbs. "How are you holding up?"

"It's been a rough twenty-four hours." What else could she say? "I'm scared. Confused. Wondering why I'm the target of these awful attacks."

A knock sounded. Jasper poked his head into the room. "Sir? The ID came through."

Chief McCoy motioned him in, and Kinsley straightened in her seat.

"What'd you find out, Holt?"

"Teddy Sayre, thirty-eight. Seven priors, mostly petty theft and robbery, not even armed. Here's the catch—he hadn't committed a crime in four years."

Chief McCoy released a rumbling, thoughtful sound. "I see."

See what? She didn't see anything except danger, all around her.

Jasper headed toward her as though reading her thoughts, his closeness a counterbalance to her erratic pulse. She'd thought he was foolish earlier, luring their pursuer after them. But he'd been right, and now there was one less man after her.

He addressed the chief. "There's something else. Mr. Sayre is also from Atlanta."

Kinsley flattened her palms on her legs and squeezed. *What?*

McCoy ran his pointer finger and thumb over his mustache repeatedly. "So, both assailants live in your hometown, and they traveled two hours to go after *you*." He cocked his head, his mild expression morphing into a hawkeyed perusal. "Any ideas why, Ms. Miller?"

"I have no idea. I'm a biologist. I study animals for a living."

"As do I," Jasper murmured.

McCoy speared him with a sharp look.

She continued. "I came back to say goodbye to my

aunt and to study gray bats in the area. That's it." She straightened in the chair. "Why do you keep asking *me* like I brought this on myself?"

Jasper's hand found her arm, offering a calming re-assurance. "Hey, I—*we*—don't mean to go after you about this. We're just trying to nail down a motive."

"Ms. Miller, my apologies. I don't think you brought this on yourself. But what we need is a lead. Some rea-son you'd possess a file or information they desperately want. Because unfortunately, the man Holt brought in—Teddy Sayre—pleaded the Fifth."

She clasped her hands. "On the way over here, I did think of one possibility—but it's out there."

"Try us," Jasper prompted.

"I have a coworker who's in the running for the same position I am at the zoo. The woman I told you about, Jasper. We make light of it at work, but I know she would really, really like that position. Marta won't be happy if I get it. However, to contradict what I just said, someone must've paid these guys, right? Marta is get-ting a divorce and doesn't have much money right now. Plus, what file would she want from me?"

McCoy scribbled some notes. "What's her name?"

"My coworker? Marta Akers. You think she could be part of this?"

Jasper sat in the chair beside hers. "I'll run back-ground checks on her. See what comes up."

Their eyes met and held. An edgy energy hummed off him, like he was ready for more of what had hap-pened earlier. How was he not exhausted like her?

Kinsley clasped her hands. "Sometime I need to get together with the funeral home director about the ser-vice next week. And I have some work to finish while

I'm here. Which means going out in the field for observation and samples."

"I don't think that's wise," Jasper answered immediately.

"You're under protective police custody, but I agree with Officer Holt. Your work will have to wait for now." McCoy regarded her for several seconds, then looked at Jasper. "Let's get Mr. Sayre's sworn statement once he's done with surgery. Comb his truck for evidence. You run background on the coworker. See what comes from that. We'll go from there."

"Yes, sir." Jasper addressed Kinsley. "I think you should stay at the cabin again."

"I did last night." She tucked in her chin. "Part of why I came was to get my dad's office cleaned out, the furniture donated and anything else in the house removed so I can finally…"

"Sell the house?" Jasper volunteered.

"Yes. Aunt Rhonda left it to me, and I can't… I don't want to live there."

"Understood." McCoy's brows hiked up. "But you can't be at your old house right now. It's an active crime scene."

"I'd prefer she stay with…out at the cabin."

She bristled as they talked around and over her. "Even though it might bring danger to your doorstep? And your son…" The thought of someone harming Gabriel Holt sent her heart into a spin cycle.

"My family will be fine. You're the one taking a risk by not consenting to stay there."

"Jasper! Don't—"

Chief McCoy held up his palms. "If Ms. Miller wants to stay in town at the Tunnel Creek Inn, that's doable. Inside entry. Should be safe. Does that work for you?"

He addressed Kinsley finally, and she nodded. "I can set up protection detail there for tonight."

She closed her eyes for a long moment. Was she being foolish? But having her own room, silence, and a good night's sleep sounded so tempting. Time to go over her notes, look through her emails. Take a hot shower... Well, sort of. Without getting her hair and face soaked.

"I can do it," Jasper said. "Hammond and I can split the shift."

Guilt was a sharp stick poking Kinsley's side. She was making Jasper's life more complicated. Taking his attention away from his family.

She addressed Chief McCoy. "I'd like to stay at the inn tonight. Thank you. Do you need anything else from me, sir?"

He gave a slow shake of his head, then stopped. "Ah, yes. Your car was brought over by Officer Hammond earlier. It's in the station parking lot."

"Thank you."

Kinsley gathered her purse—and what was left of her sanity—and exited the office, ignoring Jasper's flat-lined mouth. He wanted her to stay with him, she understood that. Understood why. But not at the expense of his family. Not at the risk of his sweet son.

She slowed in the station lobby. Should she wait for him? *Was* she taking a risk? The high-pitched hum of a printer feeding paper through its drawers and the burble of a busy Keurig interrupted her ponderings.

She was standing inside the Tunnel Creek Police Station, then she'd be staying at a hotel with inside entry and locked doors. She would be—she *was*—safe.

She repeated the mantra as she passed the receptionist desk and stepped outdoors, into the bright sunshine. How incongruous that today had been full of danger and yet the sun still shone, the scent of freshly cut grass carrying on the breeze. A bright blue dragonfly flitted past, its luminous compound eyes a balm to her nerves.

*God is always with you, sweetheart.*

Aunt Rhonda's gentle reminder during one of their last conversations. A knot formed in her throat. Rhonda's patience with her stubbornness over not returning to Tunnel Creek knotted Kinsley's stomach. Her determination to excel in her field above all else haunted her now as she considered the hours in the hotel room. Alone.

*She was safe.*

Kinsley located her car in the station lot. She patted her pockets looking for her keys, but after three seconds she stopped, gulping air. Who had the keys? Sweat prickled her brow.

"Looking for these?"

A man's voice. She whipped around to find a tall, sandy-haired officer standing a few feet away. Her keys dangled in his outstretched hand.

How had she not heard him? She grasped them carefully, her gaze jumping from the metal key chain with its Southeastern Zoo logo to the man's friendly expression.

"Thanks. Are you Officer Hammond?"

"The one and only. And you're Kinsley Miller." His grin tugged her memory.

"Thank you for bringing my car back."

"No problem." He settled back on his heels. "You doing okay? Holt said you had another rough day."

"Yes, very rough." A second pang of familiarity followed. *Déjà vu.* Kinsley eyed him closely. "Did you go to Tunnel Creek High? Wait… Dean Hammond?" He used to be whip-thin and lanky, and he'd put on quite a bit of weight in the last decade. But it had to be him.

"You remember me, Miss Science-and-Debate-Club Queen?" A pleased expression crossed Dean's round, boyish face.

*Science and Debate Club.* She shook her head. "That was a long time ago."

"I hear you're a real scientist now. Studying animals?"

"Yes, it's my passion."

"I remember when a certain officer around here was also a passion of yours." He winked, and warmth crept into Kinsley's cheeks at his teasing.

Another voice joined their conversation.

"Kinsley? You get your keys?" Jasper strode over. "Hey, Dean."

"We're good, Holt. We were just reminiscing about old times."

"I'm all set." Kinsley waved the keys in the air to show Jasper, then skated around the side of her RAV4. She unlocked it and slid in as the men continued talking.

She shut the door, then started the engine, resting her forehead to the steering wheel. Her pulse slowed to normal levels in the warm interior.

Someone knocked on the window, and she startled. *Jasper.* She set a hand on her chest before rolling down the window.

"Didn't mean to scare you."

She released a pent-up breath. "I'm really jittery these days."

"Understandable." He reached back to rub his neck in what looked like a Swedish massage of epic proportions. "Sure you won't reconsider staying at the cabin with us?"

"Maybe tomorrow." How to explain? "I'd just like a night alone. I have a couple phone calls to make."

He let go of his neck and leaned closer, filling her open window. Why did being around him make her feel jumpy *and* safe? This was not helping steady her heart rate.

"Before you head out, question. The paperwork you're going through at your parents'—I mean, your aunt's. Is it important? Can't one of those trucks just come and shred it for you?"

She buckled her seat belt. "It's my dad's old law files. Legally, I think they were supposed to be shredded within a certain number of years. Aunt Rhonda never got around to it. I need to oversee the beginning of the process at least."

Jasper's gaze locked with hers as realization trickled like hot water down her limbs.

"Files?" His Adam's apple bobbed.

"Jasper. What if that's it? Do you think the men are looking for one of those files?"

"Could be. Maybe a former client wants to make some information disappear and knew you'd be going through them soon." He tapped the top of her SUV. "We need to get those. All of them. No shredding. I'll send an officer to your house to retrieve them. Another thing. Do you mind if I take a look at your aunt's hospital records?"

"Why?" Her breaths drew shallow, and she touched the bandage. "Do you think her death wasn't an accident?"

"We have to look at all possibilities at this point."

"I trust your judgment. If you think it'll help." She licked her lips, then caught him watching. They both looked away. "Can I head over to the inn now?"

"Yes. I'm following you. I'll be on duty for part of the night, Hammond for the other. You call me or text,

I'll be there before you finish singing 'Yankee Doodle Dandy.'"

She blinked at him, fighting a smile. "Why would I sing that?"

"I don't know. Might be distracting while you're waiting for me."

He winked, reminding her of long summer evenings by the lake and carefree hikes through Sumter. She shook those memories away, waved and shifted into Reverse.

Twenty minutes later Kinsley unlocked her door on the third floor of the Tunnel Creek Inn. She lugged her suitcase inside and turned to shut and lock the door. She even shoved her suitcase in front of it. Then she washed up and changed into a pair of running shorts and a T-shirt. She took off her bandage and gaped at her reflection in the mirror. The wound was still fiery red and bruised along the outside but not quite as swollen.

After reapplying the ointment and a new bandage, Kinsley walked out of the bathroom and sat on the edge of the bed. Time to do the hard stuff. She thumbed through her phone, reaching the funeral home contact info. She dialed the number and hit Speaker, then squared her shoulders.

A young woman's voice answered, "Anderson Funeral Home. May I help you?"

"Yes, hello. This is Kinsley Miller. I'm in town and need to speak with Mr. Anderson about my aunt Rhonda's service next Saturday."

"Oh, hi, Ms. Miller."

"Please, call me Kinsley."

"Sure, will do. This is Amy, his daughter. Unfortunately, he's in a meeting with a client right now, but let me check about his plans. Hold on, please." A lengthy pause followed; then Amy came back on the line, breathless "My father said everything was set for Rhonda's service. Also, you can pick up your aunt's things anytime. Or just the day of the service."

"What things?"

"Um, let me see what the note says." Scuffling ensued for several seconds. "There's a cross-body bag—one of those big ones. Some paperwork inside. And a couple files."

"Files." Kinsley's heart swooped in her chest like a hawk on a windy day.

"Yes. We don't normally have personal items here, but one of your aunt's friends found the bag in Rhonda's car after she passed, I believe." Amy continued, "There's a large brown lockbox out back for when we're closed, and we have paperwork and items to give clients. Dad can put all the items from your aunt out there if you want. The code is seven-six-five-five."

Kinsley's blood turned to ice. She jumped up, grabbed a pen from the desk. Jotted down the number. Aunt Rhonda had had files with her—in her car—when she died. What was she going to do with them?

*These* must be the files the men were after.

# SIX

Jasper leaned his head against the headrest. The blinking lights at the Kwik Fill Station where he'd parked were giving him a headache. The Tunnel Creek Inn sat silent across the road, the lot mostly empty. It was nearly 10:00 p.m.

He cracked his back and stretched, picturing Kinsley earlier at the station. Tired. Wary. Overwhelmed. Hopefully, she could get some shut-eye. Meanwhile, he'd sleep once this case was solved. With McCoy riding his tail about possible leads and his occasional brain fogginess leftover from the Willard Tuttle incident, it felt like he was rock climbing on wet granite.

His cell buzzed. *Better not be Officer Hammond again.* Dean had texted twice already from Kinsley's old house with trivial questions. Jasper has asked Hammond to stop by the Millers' place and retrieve all the paperwork from Henry Miller's office above the garage. Hopefully something of interest would turn up.

He drew the phone from the holder, his jaw dropping.

Jasper, is that you in the parking lot? There's something I need to tell you.

His fingers flew across the screen. What's wrong?

There was an extended pause and blinking dots; she was typing a long text back to him. Finally, a response:

I found out something about a file.

His gut twisted.

I'm coming up. What's your room number?

305. Thank you.

He started up his vehicle and crossed the quiet highway. Only eight cars in the Tunnel Creek Inn parking lot. Five Georgia plates, one Ohio, one Tennessee, one Maine. He took a slow turn around the entire building, stopping at the back. Two service entrances, both appeared locked. No activity, no sign of employee movement. One passenger van sat in the farthest spot, the inn's logo on the side.

Jasper parked out front. He sent a message to Dispatch with the details, then jumped out and strode into the lobby. A dark-haired, early-twentysomething young woman slumped in the chair. Shiny nose rings and multiple earrings shone under the lights. When her zombie stare broke away from her phone and met his, her brown eyes filled her narrow face. She looked familiar, but that was normal in Tunnel Creek.

"Hello. Uh, hi?" She scuttled off her chair. "Am I in trouble? Is everything okay?"

"I'm just here to check on a hotel patron. She's in room 305." He couldn't share too many details, nor did he want the young woman to get the wrong idea about this visit. "She has some evidence for her case."

"Okay, sure." The girl fell back into her chair, then waved him toward the elevator. Her eyes dropped back to her phone.

He rode the elevator to the third floor. The hallway was deathly silent, until the hum of the ice maker cranked over as he located her room number.

Jasper knocked quietly. The lock clicked right away, like she'd been waiting right there. "Who is it?"

"Yankee Doodle Dandy."

"What's my favorite flavor of ice cream?"

Easy. "Mint chocolate chip."

Two seconds later the knob latch unlocked, and she cracked the door open with the top chain latch still attached. "You have a good memory."

*Despite the hard knock to my skull last month*, he almost blurted out.

She eyed him, then closed the door to unlatch it. When she yanked it the rest of the way open, she motioned him inside with a troubled expression.

"What happened?" He stepped through, then closed and locked the door.

She sank onto the side of the bed. Her arms twisted across her middle as she explained the call to the funeral home.

"The woman who answered the phone said I could come get her things tomorrow."

Jasper scribbled notes. For the last few hours, he'd been sure Kinsley's case was about the old law files. This was another twist. Could it all have to do with Rhonda Miller? But why? Jasper gnawed his cheek. He had not seen this one coming. And yet he'd had an itch about Rhonda's death since Kinsley's second attack. Somehow the incidents must be tied together.

"I'm coming with you to retrieve the file."

She nodded.

He sent a quick text to McCoy to let him know about the call. "We'll go tomorrow morning. What time do they open?"

Kinsley checked their website from her cell. "Not until noon." Her mouth curved down. "Do you think this is all about Aunt Rhonda? She couldn't be involved in crime. She just couldn't." A sudden sob made her words hard to understand. The urge to comfort her swamped his good sense.

"I don't know," he said, moving to her side. "But I'm going to use everything in my power to get to the bottom of this."

"I should've come back sooner." She covered her face with her hands, and he gave in. Set an arm across her back. Cupped her shoulder gently so she rested against him. Ignored how warm and familiar she felt in his half-embrace.

"Her death is not your fault."

"But…maybe I could've helped her. Saved her."

"Or gotten killed, too."

She trembled. "I'm so scared, Jasper. I don't understand why this is happening, and I hate feeling this way. I can't imagine my life ever going back to normal."

"I know things are bad now, but this is when we trust God to work out the hard details. And to keep us safe." He firmed his jaw. "Remember Mr. Avery, from tenth grade?"

She sent him a sideways look. "The math teacher whose wife was killed in a boating accident?"

Jasper grimaced. Maybe not the best example. Still,

he plowed on. "Yeah, him. Remember that picture he kept up in his classroom, the one of his wife?" She nodded, her brows crimped in confusion. "Can you recall what he hung over that picture?"

"A scripture plaque." She closed her eyes for a moment. "'Trust in the Lord with all thine heart, and lean not unto thine own understanding. In all thy ways acknowledge Him, and He shall direct thy paths.'"

"Proverbs three, five and six." He angled his face toward the ceiling. "Mom used to pray that for us when we were young. Late at night. After she'd painted for hours. She thought I was asleep, but I wasn't always. She'd come in our room at midnight. Pray that over me and Noah. Probably went into Brielle's room and did the same. I'd see the paint flecks on my blankets the next day." He met her gaze. "I do that now for Gabe, minus the paint."

"You're a wonderful dad, Jasper."

"Don't know about that. I try. Best I can figure, loving kids and praying for them is the foundation. The rest will fall into place eventually."

She smiled, and it was so soft his chest ached. "Thank you for this. I needed that reminder."

He pulled away and stood. "I'm going to head out. Thanks for letting me know about this. I'll be on duty another hour, then a different officer will keep watch. Things seem safe here." He eyed the door. "Keep that locked no matter what."

"I will. I put my suitcase in front of it, too."

He chuckled, and she smiled. "It's silly, but I feel safer."

"Okay, well. Good night."

Jasper left the hotel room. The click of the latch and

the scud of something heavy being placed in front of the door followed.

He walked to the elevator, blinking away the image of her lovely face marred by worry. Fear. Distress. Lord willing, he'd figure this out and she'd never need to block her doorway again.

Kinsley rubbed her aching temples. Jasper's presence had calmed her, but now the fear returned.

*"Trust in the Lord..."*

She shuffled to the bathroom, repeating the verse he'd reminded her of. The freckles on her nose and cheeks were more prominent because she'd cried, and the bandage stood out like an ugly white button on her hairline. She cringed. Jasper had seen her like this for the last few minutes. She needed to sleep and eat a decent meal tomorrow so she could be a help to him instead of a hindrance as he worked on her case.

She located the pain medication, popped one pill and chugged from the hotel's complimentary water bottle. Then she brushed her teeth and headed for the bed.

Three minutes later she gave in to the drowsiness tugging at her eyelids.

Kinsley jerked awake from a heavy sleep. Darkness enveloped her, and an alarm blared so loud goosebumps broke out on her arms. Where was she? *The Tunnel Creek Inn.* What was happening? Her pulse roared through her ears as she sat up. Was that the hotel fire alarm?

She lurched out of bed and stumbled toward the door. Shoving at the suitcase, she stood, chest heaving. Wasn't she supposed to go to the stairwell if there was a fire?

Kinsley bit the inside of her cheek and waited. The alarm continued ringing. She fumbled with the locks, then pulled the door open as the angry warning light flashed bloodred across her vision.

A man in a black ski mask loomed in the hallway, his wide shoulders and chilling blue eyes focused on her. Like he'd been waiting for her.

"No!" A scream throttled her throat, but the sound was lost to the shrieking fire alarm.

He lunged forward, draping her mouth with a dirty rag. The stench of chemicals mixed with terror was her last thought as shadows claimed her consciousness.

# SEVEN

Jasper exited the cabin at a dead sprint toward the Charger. Dash launched into the vehicle first; then he folded himself inside and slammed the door. It was 5:10 a.m., and the call from McCoy had shocked him out of a dead sleep.

"Ms. Miller was kidnapped from the inn a few minutes ago. Hammond wasn't on scene. Someone pulled the fire alarm. She was gone when the firemen checked the rooms." The chief's apologetic tone had Jasper even more riled.

But there wasn't any point in laying blame. What good would it do now, anyway?

*God, please protect Kinsley. Lay breadcrumbs for us, please.*

Jasper flew into town, arriving at the inn seven minutes later. Seven minutes too long. He pulled up next to Officer Matt Reed. "Chief got a tip from someone on Danley Lane. Saw the stolen hotel van out near Sumter Road. Near the old glass warehouse?"

*Thank You, Lord.* The town-wide text-alert system was paying off when it mattered most.

"Got it. Where's Hammond?" Jasper asked.

"Said he was called away to a possible home invasion on Ninth Street at four-forty-five. He's just finishing up."

Jasper growled under his breath. Timed on purpose, no doubt.

"You have your partner?" Matt peered into Jasper's car.

"Dash is here. Can they trace her phone?"

"No. She left it on the nightstand." Matt leaned out his window. "Here, I brought one of her shirts for Dash."

"Thanks." He retrieved the scrap of clothing his partner would use to track Kinsley. "Anything missing from her room?"

"Nothing that I could tell. I'll dust for prints, in case. Firemen found an alarm pulled in the employee wing. Front desk clerk was in hysterics. She fell asleep during her shift."

Jasper scowled. None of this news helped.

"Look, man," Matt said, "you go on. I'll wait for the chief. ETA, six minutes."

Jasper nodded affirmatively. He checked for traffic and peeled out of the parking lot. The last shadows of night cloaked the area, offering only patches of fog and the blank faces of mostly dark houses. Few people were up at this hour.

His phone buzzed. "Holt here."

"Jasper, what's this I hear about a kidnapping?"

David Barnhill. Great. Now he'd be answering not only to Chief McCoy but also the mayor, who made it a point to know everything that happened in Tunnel Creek. Even more than Jasper did. While he respected the elder man's care for the town, right now it felt like an added chink in Jasper's failing armor.

"Yes, sir. Ms. Kinsley Miller was abducted from the

Tunnel Creek Inn approximately fifteen minutes ago. We're taking care of the situation."

"This is terrible. Is she a tourist? Hiker?"

"No, sir. She's the young lady who used to live here. A former classmate of mine. She's in town for her aunt's memorial. Rhonda Miller." He left off the *studying bats* part.

"I see. Do you have any clues to her whereabouts? We can't have another murder like…"

Jasper swallowed what felt like a mouthful of glass. *Willard Tuttle's.* Like he needed the reminder. "I agree, sir. I will do everything in my power to find her."

"Excellent. I know you will."

Jasper tapped the wheel as the mayor talked about an upcoming event at the city park. How much security they'd need. Stuff they could discuss later, when Kinsley's life wasn't on the line. He flicked on his turn signal and panned both sides of the road. The mayor's words blurred into extraneous sound. He was nearing Sumter Road now, and the houses had disappeared, leaving large clusters of dark woods and foggy fields as the forest boundary met the town limit. Was Kinsley at the abandoned warehouse? Dread writhed down his spine. He'd been up there a couple of times, kicking out teens skipping school or acting out dares during the boring days of summer.

The mayor cleared his throat, and Jasper snapped to attention. "I don't like this, Holt. People are going to feel unsafe if we don't catch this fellow. I'm counting on you to do that."

"I'll do my best." It was more like *fellows.* Which was still too nice of a term for the criminals they were dealing with. He ended the call and tapped the brakes.

His headlights illuminated a crooked square white sign that read "Sumter Glassworks."

Jasper parked off the side of the road leading to the glass factory, then cut the lights. Backup would arrive in minutes. He surveyed the surroundings, then unfolded from the Charger, flashlight and handheld radio in his grip. Dash's reward stuffed animal, Rocky, was shoved in his back pocket.

He circled the vehicle, then opened the driver-side door. Dash barreled out, tail high and bulletproof vest snugly wrapping his lean frame. Jasper held his hand out, and the dog butted his cold, wet nose against his palm. Once. Twice.

His partner was ready.

"Hey, boy." He held out an article of Kinsley's clothing from her hotel room. Her shirt from yesterday, the scent of lemons clinging to it. "Seek. Seek Kinsley."

The dog sniffed the material, then trotted in the direction of the immense white-and-gray warehouse. Jasper followed.

*There.* Fresh tire tracks marred the damp dirt of the factory's driveway. Why had she been brought back here?

*Please, God, lead me to her.*

Broken windows glinted from the second floor, and two sets of double doors sat on either side of the building, one hanging open. Overgrown shrubs hugged the sidewalk leading to the doors, and tree branches scraped the building in the breeze.

A single light hung near one of the double doors, the last remaining trace of the once-active business. Written across the large window beside one of the double doors—probably the front-office area—a sign warned, "Stay Out, Private Property."

Jasper came alongside Dash, who sniffed the ground near the walkway. He offered the shirt again, asked him to seek. Dash snuffled the material, then thrust his nose into the knee-high grass and stones littering the front of the building.

Jasper crept beside him, flashlight on dim. A crackle on the handheld three-way radio broke the eerie silence.

Linda's voice: "Location? Over."

"Forest Road. Glass warehouse. Over."

"Copy. Any sign of kidnapping victim?"

"Negative. Dash is working. Over."

Jasper turned down the small radio before proceeding, his boots crushing weeds and damp earth. Dash stopped, his muzzle buried in a cluster of what appeared to be wildflowers and grass. Then he sat, looking back at Jasper.

Jasper shot forward with electrified limbs.

A piece of white material lay on the ground, partially hidden. A sock? Had Kinsley been wearing socks? He pictured her sitting on the hotel bed... Yes. White ankle socks with little yellow chicks on them. He aimed the light on the small article of clothing.

Same sock.

"Thank You, God." At least they were on track. She had to be nearby. But where was the white van he'd seen—and more importantly, where was Kinsley?

He combined the sock and the shirt and asked Dash to sniff them again. "Dash, seek. Seek!"

The dog set off straight toward the door. Jasper trailed behind, one hand on his weapon and the other holding the flashlight. A chorus of crickets covered their silent pursuit.

Dash darted through the doorway, then paused on the inside. Sniffed the air, snuffed the ripped-up floors.

Then he trotted forward, down a long hallway that ran to the back of the warehouse. Jasper ventured after him, the scent of mildew and moldy food stinging his nose.

Dash disappeared into a corridor, and Jasper followed, his eyes adjusting to the unlit building. Boxes, old equipment, chairs piled atop desks. Even a discarded cooler lined the hallway. Where was Kinsley?

The crunching ping of tires kicking up gravel jerked his head around. Where…? Jasper ducked, weapon drawn, searching for a window. He took the corridor until he passed a room with outside windows. Edging into the darkened space, he peered out. A narrow service road led around the side and back of the warehouse. No sign of the vehicle he'd just heard.

His muscles went taut. Had the kidnapper taken her somewhere else?

Dash whined from several yards away. Jasper darted through the doorway and followed the sound down the corridor. Then a muffled feminine cry carried through the eerie silence.

*Kinsley!* He shot forward. At the far end of the hallway, Dash sat on his haunches and looked straight at a closed door marked "Storage" as Jasper approached.

"Good boy."

He tossed Dash his squirrel, Rocky, then opened the door, weapon trained. *Please, God…*

Kinsley lay sideways, shoved inside the small space like an oversize doll. Ankles and wrists duct-taped. Her hair haloed her head, and an angry slash of silver tape covered her mouth. Relief buzzed in his ears. Her damp, red eyes and the evidence of her rough treatment sent a lightning bolt through him.

*Calm down, Holt. She's alive.*

He knelt in front of the open closet. "Hey, I'm here. I've got you."

He reached for her, hating that he had to hurt her. She nodded encouragement, and he clenched his jaw, then yanked the tape from her mouth. She flinched, but instead of relief, a frantic fire filled her eyes.

"Jasper," she panted. "The inn… A fire alarm. I had to…" She coughed. "There's s—"

"It's okay. I've got you."

"No, listen. The m-man talked about leaving a present for us. It sounded…b-bad. He was talking on the phone and s-said it was easier this way."

*A present?* The hairs on his neck rose. He stood and spun around just as Dash dropped Rocky and let out a short, sharp bark. A warning.

Jasper scrutinized the immediate vicinity. What was that? He stepped across the hall.

A black backpack lay on the floor of what looked like a break room. Directly across from the closet where she'd been dumped. Wires spread out from the half-zipped opening, and an unmistakable *tick, tick, tick* scorched his ears.

His blood turned to acid. A bomb.

Kinsley gulped in a lungful of musty air. Dash returned to the closet and pressed against her, whining around the raggedy brown stuffed squirrel he'd retrieved that now hung from his muzzle. She set her forehead to his muscular neck as stars dotted her peripheral vision. She'd barely been getting enough oxygen with the tape over her mouth, and when her abductor had shut the closet door, panic set in. Then it became even harder to breathe.

Jasper whistled at Dash to move. The iron bands of

his arms slipped under her, freeing her from the awful closet that felt like a tomb. He clutched her to his chest; then the world spun. They were running down a corridor, pain jarring her skull and jaw with each stride. Her thoughts foundered.

Why was he running? What had he found?

Jasper's pounding footsteps and harsh breaths matched her galloping heartbeat. He shouted something to someone up ahead. Dash's sleek brown-and-black form loped just ahead of them. Bright lights shone through the corridor as they neared a double door... An exit?

Then they were through it.

Everything went silent for a split second; then she and Jasper were flying forward. She screamed as heat licked up her arms, crimped her eyelashes and eyebrows. The flying sensation stopped. They landed with a jarring thud, Kinsley still clasped in Jasper's arms.

Had a bomb just exploded?

Dirt and leaves stuck to her face, and something hard poked her calf. A rock. They were lying on the ground outside the building. Waves of pain radiated off the wound on her forehead, and the rhythmic thumping of a human heart filtered through her shock. But... not her own.

"Jasper?" She blinked away the smoke filling her vision, burning her eyes and nose. The kidnapper must've left a bomb. But they were alive. What if Jasper had gotten there two minutes later? Her eyes smarted.

*Thank You, Lord.*

"Jasper, are you okay?" Was she—she lay half-across him, one of her elbows near his throat. Her wrists were still taped together. Dash stood over them, muzzle gripping the stuffed squirrel. The dog dropped the stuffed animal, then licked Jasper's ear.

"Urgh. Dash, quit."

She struggled upright and then gasped. Blood poured down his temple and over his ear where Dash was nudging him.

"Jasper! You're bleeding."

"It's just a superficial cut." He tried to stand but wobbled midmovement, one palm jammed to the ground as though he was dizzy.

"How do you know it's superficial?"

"I'm alive, aren't I?" His mouth quirked on one side in a weak smile.

"Stop joking. Hold still." She searched awkwardly for the wound with her bound hands. There, on his upper skull—a small laceration. Sticky warmth coated his hair, and she pressed the heel of her palm to the wound to staunch the flow. *The tape.* With effort, she wriggled her wrists the rest of the way apart, then tore off the hem of her shirt. "I'm going to try and stop the blood." Kinsley put the cloth to the wound and pressed down hard. Dash paced in circles around them as though checking to make sure she was doing it right.

Jasper groaned.

Sirens carried through the woods. Moments later, footsteps announced another person's arrival. Chief McCoy was striding their way, his severe expression emphasized by the flashing blue and red lights from the police cars behind him.

"Get the paramedics down here. Now!" Chief barked at someone standing out of sight. "Holt, what on earth happened in there?"

Jasper's muscles tensed against her. "A bomb." He gingerly pushed himself to standing. She did the same, keeping close in case he wobbled again. Which he did, twice.

"What do you know?" his superior asked.

"I spoke to Ms. Miller at approximately ten p.m., interviewing her about her call to the funeral home. That's when I notified you. Then I left. My shift ended at midnight. Officer Hammond took my place, but he was called away to a possible home invasion at four forty-five a.m. The inn's fire alarms were tripped just before five a.m., and we believe during that time, she was abducted. The firemen checked her room and found it empty."

Chief McCoy released a frustrated growl, then met Kinsley's gaze. "It appears we'll need another statement."

She nodded, her throat like sandpaper.

Chief pointed at Jasper's head. "And you need to get that looked at. That's your second head injury in five weeks." He stroked his mustache, staring off into space. "Maybe we should get another officer on Ms. Miller's case so you can rest?"

Kinsley bit her lower lip to keep from arguing about the chief's observation. She didn't trust anyone besides Jasper.

"No. Please, I'm fine, sir."

"You're one of my best officers, Holt. But your head isn't going to get any better if you continue putting yourself in harm's way." He glared at the destroyed building. "I've wanted this place closed up for good, but this wasn't the way I'd hoped to do it." He addressed Kinsley. "Did you happen to see the vehicle, Ms. Miller?"

"No," Kinsley murmured. Whatever drug the masked man had given her had knocked her out and impaired her observational skills.

Chief McCoy's attention strayed back to the demolished building. "We've got all roads blocked in the immediate area. If that van turns up, we'll be right on it."

"I think we need to canvass the area, and it might be a good idea for the team of divers from Greenville PD to check the lake behind the factory. See if the van was dumped there."

Chief waved a hand. "We'll do that if the weather holds up. Last I heard, we have a major storm system coming through tomorrow evening. The dive team's safety comes first."

"Of course."

Chief McCoy continued, "Mayor Barnhill wants this case solved ASAP. And he's breathing down my neck about it. You're sure you can handle this?"

"Yes, sir." Jasper sent a fleeting look her way.

An hour later Kinsley sat in nearly the same spot as the night before, wearing another itchy hospital gown and waiting inside an ice cube of a room.

Noah Holt had taken Dash home before they loaded into the ambulance. Kinsley yawned at the beeping heart and O2 monitors hooked up to her body. They'd run more tests; rebandaged her tender, reopened wound, along with a small laceration on her arm from the explosion; and announced she was healthy. She sure didn't *feel* healthy.

By the time she'd changed and Jasper joined her, leading her back to his vehicle wearing his own bandage above his left eyebrow, her eyelids drooped.

She buckled her seat belt with a yawn. A question nagged her hazy thoughts like a flickering light bulb on a foggy morning. While she'd waited to see a doctor for her wounds, she'd overheard a physician questioning Jasper in the next room. Words like *double vision* and *forgetfulness* carried through the ER exam room's thin walls.

"What happened that everyone is so worried about your head?"

He started the vehicle and pulled out of the parking lot. "I was injured on the job a few weeks ago."

"Do you want to talk about it?"

"Not really."

She was surprised at how much his refusal stung. "And now my situation is causing more problems for you. Making it worse." Her voice cracked. "I'm sorry about all this."

"It's not your fault, Kinsley." He steered onto the main road, eyes straight ahead, expression somber. "I'm trying to do my job to the best of my ability."

"And I'm grateful for that." She massaged her temples, cautious of her bandage. "I should've stayed at the cabin."

He shrugged.

She lay her head against the headrest. "I just wanted to say goodbye to Aunt Rhonda and study bats. That was it."

"And I just want to keep my town safe and free of crime." He pulled up to stoplight and looked her way. "So, why bats?"

Telling him felt like handing over a piece of her heart. "They remind me of my dad."

He snorted softly. "How so?"

"Before Dad started his own law firm and life got so busy, we'd go for these long hikes together." Memories seared the back of her eyes. "Dad is the one who first took me to the Whisper Mountain Tunnel. One day, when we were leaving, he thought he saw a bat come out of it. I mean, we'd see bats at twilight sometimes, out in the forest, but this one flew right over us. Dad explained how important they are for the environment. He made it...interesting. I was scared of them before, and he took that fear away."

"He was a nice guy, and so protective of you. I remember getting the stink eye from him before our dates."

She grinned. "Didn't he show you his knife collection once?"

"Sure did. Every single one. Even the utility knives." He glanced her way again, his smile joining hers. "Maybe this is out of line, but I'm proud of you." He stared back at the road. "And they'd be proud of you. You dealt with some tough stuff, but you pushed through. Finished college. Accomplished your goals. Now you're living your dream, making a difference."

Warmth bloomed on her cheeks. "Thank you. I am kind of obsessed with making sure animal populations survive and flourish."

"I can see that." He slowed at a four-way stop sign but stayed put, eyes glued to the rearview mirror.

"What're you doing?"

"Making sure we weren't tailed."

A chill slithered down her limbs as they waited. Once he was satisfied there was no one following them, he steered the vehicle through the intersection.

"Does your mom mind living out here with you guys?"

"Are you kidding? She gets her grandson 24/7 and her own art studio. And I get homecooked meals and cheese sculptures." He guffawed then grew serious. "A little while after my wife left and we divorced, my mom had some financial difficulties. It worked out that we both benefited from her moving into the cabin." He exhaled. "Still, it was a rough time. Michelle had struggled with being a mom since Gabe was born."

"In what way? Feeling tied down?"

"Partly that. Mostly because she didn't really want kids." He whispered, and the intimate setting of the vehicle emphasized the admission.

"How can you not love that sweet little boy?"

"I know, right?" Silence ensued, and Kinsley didn't push him to share more.

"Michelle was an actress," he murmured. "Plays, theater, all that. Full of life and fire." He scrubbed a palm across his face. "It was a fireworks relationship."

"Fireworks relationship?"

He chuckled, the sound heavy when it should've been light. "We were colorful together, had fun—until it wasn't, and I realized all there was between us was a lot of smoke and noise. We met at Clemson senior year and hit it off. She liked that I was going into law enforcement. But I think she pictured *NYPD Blue* or something exciting like that. She didn't want to move to a Podunk town like Tunnel Creek, and I couldn't see living somewhere else. So she returned home to Charlotte, and I came back here. We saw each other on weekends." He bumped the back of his skull into the headrest. "I didn't live a perfect life. There were…mistakes made."

*At least you didn't kill your parents.*

Jasper's head jerked around to face her. "What?"

Had she said that out loud? "Nothing. It's…nothing. Go on." *Not* going down that path.

He continued, his low voice rumbling through the vehicle. "The weekend I was going to end the relationship—after two years of dating—she told me she was pregnant. So we got married and she moved here. Hated every second. She left when Gabriel was four and a half, and she'd see him from time to time. Last year, Michelle died in an accident after one of her performances. She was driving drunk and hit a bridge."

"That's terrible."

"To this day…" His words shifted from solid to liquid. Concrete to sand. "I'm not sure Gabriel's mine. But I don't care because in here, he is." He pressed a fist to his heart. "He *is* my son."

She covered his hand with hers. "It's obvious how much you love him. I'm sure he knows that, and it's all that matters."

"I hope so." He flexed his hands and, in doing so, pulled away from her.

She sat up, her palm still warm. Clearly, he didn't want her comfort. Kinsley tried to shake off the hurt.

They made their way inside, greeted by the two boisterous hounds and the alert shepherd. Dash trotted over and sniffed Jasper, as though checking to make sure he hadn't missed any additional action after coming home with Noah.

Dana Holt stood in the living room, surrounded by the canine fray. "Jasper Holt, what's this I hear about a bomb?" Her face was tangled with worry. "Kinsley, are you okay?"

"I'm exhausted but safe. Thanks to Jasper." Dana's features straightened out, maternal pride shining from her eyes. "Now I'd like to sleep for twenty-four hours."

"That's perfectly fine. Do either of you need anything?"

"How about a boring day in Tunnel Creek?" He slipped off his boots.

"Your head…" his mom murmured, stepping closer. "Did you sustain another—"

"I'm okay." He cut off her question but allowed her

to check his wound, and she *tsk*ed and flitted around like a mother hen.

"Well, I'm sorry you had a rough night. Again." Dana ran her paint-flecked nails along her collarbone. "There's half a mozzarella turtle, if you'd like some cheese and crackers? Noah ate the shell, and Gabe had the tail." She waved her fingers in the air as an apology. "I'll be up at seven with breakfast."

Kinsley side-eyed Jasper, and they both tamped down smiles. "For now, I'd just like to sleep. Thank you anyway."

A minute later she was settled back in the bedroom she'd used the night before. She sank into the mattress and fisted a fluffy pillow. If only she'd stayed here again, like he'd wanted her to, then none of this would've happened. Unless they would've come after her *here*?

She tucked her lips to her teeth. *Gabriel.* Everything about her situation was putting Jasper and his family at risk.

Jasper stole in after her, his large frame filling the space. "Do you need anything else?" He went to the window, checked the locks and pulled the curtains closed.

*Peace that passes all understanding.* Oh, how she longed for peace. When was the last time she'd truly felt peaceful? Back home in Atlanta, in her apartment, or was it over ten years ago, before mom and dad were gone?

"I'm fine, thank you."

"From my limited experience with women, *fine* is code for 'I'm upset, but leave me alone anyway.'"

She bristled. "What if I *am* fine?"

"Then I'll leave you to get some rest." He escaped to the door.

"Jasper, wait."

He stopped in the hallway, turned. His dark eyes fell on her, weariness oozing from their golden-flecked depths.

"Sorry. I shouldn't have snapped just now." She motioned at herself. "Being here, causing all these problems for you. I wasn't even going to get in touch with… Well, I didn't mean for you to be wrapped up in this. With me. Again." What a mess she made of that apology.

"Rewind. You were going to come to Tunnel Creek, go to your aunt's service, do your study in the Whisper Mountain Tunnel and then leave without even saying *hello*?"

She tucked her shoulders. "And write the first draft of my research article in there sometime before I left. But yes."

"So you would've stayed one, two weeks?"

Her mouth dried out, and she licked her lips. "More like three weeks. Although that depended on what I found in the tunnel."

"And in that amount of time, you didn't expect to run into me in town? See me around Tunnel Creek? Didn't think I'd want to meet up, say hi, give you a hug?"

*A hug.* She immediately transported to earlier that evening, when he'd lifted her from that horrible closet and hugged her to him before taking off. How…right it felt. Familiar yet new.

She shook off the memory. "I didn't think you'd want to see me. We didn't exactly end our relationship on good terms."

"*I* didn't end it. *You* did."

"Which is exactly why I was certain you wouldn't want to see me."

He set one hand on the doorframe, leaning, and she tugged her eyes away from the masculine vision. Strong. Protective. Caring.

She couldn't let these thoughts knock on the door of her mind. Her apartment was in Atlanta; her place, at the zoo; her mission, to study the animals that needed a voice. Tunnel Creek only offered a window into her painful past and a dull ache in her chest.

He removed his hand and stood up straight. "You're wrong, you know."

"About…"

"I would've wanted to see you, get an update on your life, even if none of this happened."

He turned and disappeared down the hall, leaving her only with the sound of his retreating footsteps and an unexpected peppering of regret in her stomach.

# EIGHT

Jasper rubbed the heels of his palms into his eye sockets as he exited his room the next morning. Didn't help. He headed into the kitchen, a restless-night's sleep dragging him down like fifty extra pounds on his frame. Eight fifteen. He'd let himself sleep too long. Not that he'd actually slept much. Images of Kinsley bound and gagged on the warehouse floor had plagued his every thought—even his dreams when he did drift off.

He shook them away. His mom crisscrossed the kitchen, softly banging pots and pans. She was an early riser, doing her devotions and often painting before he and Gabe woke up.

His son sat at the table, mixing his scrambled eggs into a small pool of maple syrup.

"Daddy!"

"Gabe!" He ruffled his son's hair, squinting. The kitchen's bright overhead light and the sun streaming through the large picture window temporarily blinded him.

"Morning, Mom." He couldn't quite set *good* before it, given all that had happened in the last forty-eight hours.

"Did you sleep, honey?" She puttered over in her

# More to Love.
# More to Explore.

With more to explore, we'd love to send you up to 4 BOOKS, absolutely FREE when you try the Harlequin Reader Service.

They say that "less is more" — but not when it comes to reading your favorite books!

We know that readers like you can't wait to open their newest book and settle down reading.

We feel the same way. That's why today, you can say "YES" to MORE of the great reading you love — absolutely FREE!

Try **Love Inspired® Romance Larger-Print** and get 2 books and fall in love with inspirational romances that take you on an uplifting journey of faith, forgiveness and hope.

Try **Love Inspired® Suspense Larger-Print** and get 2 books where courage and optimism unite in stories of faith and love in the face of danger.

Or **TRY BOTH** and get 2 books from each series!

Your free books are completely free, even the shipping! If you continue with your subscription, you can look forward to curated monthly shipments of brand-new books from your selected series, always at a discount off the cover price! Plus you can cancel any time.

So don't miss out, return your Free Books Claim Card today to get your Free books.

*Pam Powers*

# Free Books Claim Card
## Say "Yes" to More Books!

▼ DETACH AND MAIL CARD TODAY! ▼

**YES! I love reading, please send me more books from the series I'd like to explore and a free gift from each series I select.**

Get MORE to read, MORE to love, MORE to explore!

Just write in **"YES"** on the dotted line below then select your series and return this Claim Card today and we'll send your free books & gift asap!

➡ *YES* ⬅

Which do you prefer?

☐ **Love Inspired®**
**Romance**
**Larger-Print**
122/322 IDL GRC6

☐ **Love Inspired®**
**Suspense**
**Larger-Print**
107/307 IDL GRC6

☐ **BOTH**
122/322 & 107/307
IDL GRDU

FIRST NAME

LAST NAME

ADDRESS

APT.#

CITY

STATE/PROV.

ZIP/POSTAL CODE

EMAIL ☐ Please check this box if you would like to receive newsletters and promotional emails from Harlequin Enterprises ULC and its affiliates. You can unsubscribe anytime.

LI/LiS-622-LR_MMM22

**BUSINESS REPLY MAIL**
FIRST-CLASS MAIL    PERMIT NO. 717    BUFFALO, NY

POSTAGE WILL BE PAID BY ADDRESSEE

**HARLEQUIN READER SERVICE**
PO BOX 1341
BUFFALO NY 14240-8571

NO POSTAGE
NECESSARY
IF MAILED
IN THE
UNITED STATES

*Starry Night* slippers and dark blue robe, wrapping him in a brief coffee-scented hug. His thoughts reversed to last night, when he'd clutched Kinsley to his chest before the bomb went off.

He flexed his jaw. *No way.* He'd tried marriage once, and he wasn't doing it again. Even if he met someone who wanted to be married and stay here, it wasn't the right time.

Guilt reared its familiar head. Even if Gabriel kept begging for a mommy.

What had his mom asked?

"I slept. Kind of," he answered.

She drilled him with knowing, worried eyes.

"Yeah, not really. But at least I stayed in bed and pretended."

"You two needed rest, and it sounds like neither of you got it."

"Kinsley is awake?" He'd assumed she wouldn't join them for another half hour at least.

"Oh yes, she was up when I got up." She padded over to the sink.

Which meant *early.* Was Kinsley that much of an early riser, too, or had sleep eluded her as well? She must've gone back to her room, then.

His mom sank a pan into the soapy water. "I'm heading into town to get painting supplies and groceries before traffic picks up. Gabe's coming with me. Noah left for work."

Jasper gave an absent nod. Had Kinsley lain awake, plagued by visions of the exploding warehouse, too? Would she be able to recall any details about her captor? Lord willing, something would come up when they got her statement later.

"Earth to Jasper. Son. Do. You. Need. Anything? Coffee?"

"Uh, no. I mean—yes, coffee. Thanks." He gripped the offered mug. "Did Kinsley eat already?"

"She grabbed an apple before she went outside."

He slapped the mug back on the counter. Coffee overflowed the top. "She went outside?"

She narrowed her eyes at the mess then stalked over to wipe the spill. "Kinsley asked to see my art studio. To do so, she'd need to walk outside."

Gabe burst past them, mumbled, "Thank you, Gwama," and then disappeared down the hall.

"Wash your hands," she called out to Gabe, then met Jasper's eye. "The studio is a stone's throw down the hill. I'm sure she's fine."

"I really don't want her going outside without me." He gulped down more coffee, then strode across the kitchen. At the far end of the room, a large basket stuffed full of shoes sat by the back door. He pulled out his boots. "There are people trying to kill her."

"She's on Holt property. Who's going to trespass here?"

He understood that line of thinking. Totally got it. That's why he'd brought Kinsley here in the first place. But still. "We're right next to a national forest. There are thousands of acres and dozens of trails where a person can creep up on our land." He shoved his feet into the shoes and grabbed his weapon from the locked cabinet beside the back door.

"When did she go to your studio?"

"About fifteen minutes ago. Calm down. She has Dash with her, son."

Okay. At least there was that. Dash would protect her and make his presence known to any dangerous people. But it wasn't a guarantee of safety. A dog wasn't a shield.

"There's an egg sandwich for you." She motioned toward the remaining frying pan and the English muffin enclosing cheesy scrambled eggs. His stomach growled.

He snatched the food and wolfed it down with a muttered "Thanks," much like his son had. Holstering his Glock beneath his T-shirt, he set off toward the restored garage slash barn that served as Mom's art studio. The dogs swarmed his legs, but he told them to stay. One dog was enough. Outside, he surveyed the property. All was quiet and still, even the birds. Noah's truck was gone, and Mom would be leaving soon with Gabe. The sun was already climbing the summer sky, glaring at him as he rushed downhill. Thick, humid air warned of stormy weather to come.

He opened the studio door.

"Jasper?" Kinsley poked her head out from behind one of his mom's larger canvases, her wavy strawberry blond hair falling over her shoulders. She yielded a paintbrush like a magic wand. A rainbow of paint speckles covered the smock she wore over her T-shirt and jean shorts.

Dash trotted over.

He shut the door and rubbed Dash's ears. "You're painting?"

"I'm *trying* to paint. I thought it would be an excellent distraction." Her smile faltered. "I couldn't sleep last night."

"Me either." He patted Dash once more, then shoved his hands into his pockets. "Is it working out?" He motioned at her.

Her eyes rounded into blue orbs in her face. "Is what working out? Us?"

He cleared his throat. *Us.* Was she referencing their conversation last night? "I meant the painting. Is it distracting you?"

"Oh. Yes, it's very relaxing."

"Huh. That's good. When Gabe paints, shirts get ruined and dogs end up with green tails. He might be relaxed, but I'm not."

"Ha. Kids need that creative outlet. My parents let me paint on our back deck."

"I'm just glad my mom handles most of that." He thrust his chin toward the canvas. "Can I see it?"

Her mouth twisted sideways. "It's not done. And it's messy."

"Hey, I can't even draw stick figures."

"Okay. But don't judge my lack of artistic ability."

He set a palm to his chest in mock hurt. "I wouldn't dare."

"You might start judging once you see this."

"Nah. You have other skills, anyway, Doctor Dolittle." Curiosity propelled his steps. When he stood beside her, surprise clocked him a good one. "Kins— is that...?"

Soft pink color covered her cheeks. "It's Gabe. And Lizzy, behind the cabin the other day." She pointed. "Gabe's not done yet, but the lizard—"

"Looks so real I've got goose bumps." He pretended to shiver. "You're pretty good at drawing animals."

Her head tilted sideways. "I've had a lot of practice over the years." She frowned. "I need to fix Gabe's hair. And his arms. They look like twigs. People are tough to draw."

"People are tough in general." He blew out a raspberry, then grinned at her. A spark lit between their gazes, squarely in the middle. His stomach muscles tightened. How had he gotten in such close proximity to her? They were only a foot apart. Sunlight shone through the window, highlighting the blue in her eyes and the curve of her mouth.

"I'd like to go back to the tunnel before we go to the funeral home."

Her words were ice water down his back. "Not happening."

"Just listen. Please."

He spread his arms out to show he was receptive to hearing her out, even though his brain already didn't agree and he was pretty certain her words would not convince him to change his mind. A skill he'd practiced often as an officer of the law.

"I remembered another detail from the night of my first attack. I had a small recording device on me when I reached the tunnel. It was in my hand because I'd planned on recording the bats when they left the tunnel at dusk. They make a high-pitched sound that's decipherable—"

"Officer Hammond checked the area, and he never found a small device."

"I'm not surprised. It's small, slightly larger than a child's coloring marker. It could've rolled underneath leaves or gotten covered with mud or sticks. Since we're close, why don't we look for it before we go to Anderson's for the file?"

He drilled his chin to his chest. "Bad idea."

"Just to take a look?"

He shook his head, jaw tightening. "No."

She set the paintbrush on the easel shelf with a solid *whack*. Clearly, she was not happy with his decision.

"Have you forgotten what happened last night? And the day before that?"

"I haven't forgotten. But if we check and see—"

"No! Drop it, Kinsley. You can do your science-y stuff when this case is solved."

"This isn't about that." Kinsley turned away, closing paint containers with sharp snaps.

She could be mad all she wanted. His job was to keep her out of harm's way while he figured out who was after her. In the irate silence, his thoughts dialed back to what she'd started to say last night in his car. Something about her parents' accident. Did she blame herself?

"Tell me about your parents' accident."

She startled. "What does that have to do with anything?"

"Maybe nothing. But it sounded like you felt...guilty. My understanding of your parents' accident was that it was exactly that—an *accident*."

"Leave it alone, Jasper."

"I'd like to hear the details."

"Just drop it." She turned to face him. "Please."

He did, but next time he was at the station, he'd be pulling the files. Checking the details himself. Just to make sure there wasn't a tie with the accident and her aunt Rhonda's death. Because he'd believed that was an accident until two days ago, and now...

Now he wondered what secrets the Miller family held close. And he couldn't exactly share that with her.

They walked back inside the house, Kinsley's quick strides bringing her ahead of him. She ascended the stairs like lava was licking at her heels. Maybe he'd been too harsh with her, but this case needled him sideways. She couldn't take undue risks, and they needed that file.

Mom met him in the entryway, a bouncy Gabe at her side. She glanced up the stairs.

"I know an upset female when I see one. Did you make fun of her painting?"

"I wouldn't do that! And why do you assume *I* did something wrong?"

"Women's intuition." She addressed Gabe. "Go grab your thermos from the kitchen so you'll have water when we're in town."

His son skipped down the hall, and Jasper folded and refolded his hands like Gabe did when he played with Play-Doh.

"She wants to go to the tunnel to look for something she dropped."

"And you're not allowed to escort her there?"

"*I'm* allowed, but I don't want *her* going."

"Ah, I see."

He kept his eyes from rolling by sheer will. Mom was often right—he'd give her that—but it didn't diminish the annoyance when she *was* right. "See what?"

"'Grow in grace,' Jasper." She tapped her colorful nails together. *Click, click.* "You can't control the situation, so you're controlling the person involved in the situation."

"I'm trying to keep her safe."

"She'll be safe if she's with you, correct?"

"Of course." Hopefully. And that was the crux of the issue.

Gabe returned, sipping from his LEGO thermos like a man lost in the desert for days. Mom clucked at him. "Gabe, that sounds empty. Go refill it please—then go potty."

"Yesh, Gwama," he whined before disappearing into the kitchen once more, confirming that Grandma—Mom—was indeed always right.

She stepped forward suddenly, her palm cradling

Jasper's cheek in a brief, tender touch. "I love you, young man. You always try to do what's right. But sometimes you have to let people outside the boundaries you set for them because *that's* right, too."

"Yesh, ma'am," he echoed like Gabe had moments ago.

He waited at the front door as she left with Gabe two minutes later, then lit up the stairs. Kinsley's door was halfway shut, and the swish of pages filled the hall. He knocked on the doorframe.

"Can I come in?"

"What is it?"

He pushed inside, dropping the scowl he wore, because that wouldn't help anything. His thoughts tumbled away at the adorable sight of her sitting cross-legged on the bed, a large art book split open on her lap.

Why wouldn't his tongue unglue from the roof of his mouth? Pride. That was it. Apologizing wasn't on his top-ten list of Fun Things to Do.

"So, uh… Sometimes I can be a little bossy. I'm sorry. We can take a quick look at the tunnel." The words rushed out in a jumble. "See if the recording device turns up."

She closed the book with a soft *whack*. "Are you sure you're allowed?"

"Yes." He unclenched his jaw. He'd send a text to McCoy to let him know what was up. "The tunnel is closed right now, but we can take a look. You just have to do what I ask when we're there."

Her features relaxed, and she stood. "We don't have to stay long. Let's just make sure it wasn't accidentally missed by the other officer. Maybe there's audio that can help with the case."

"Right. After we check the tunnel, we're heading

to Anderson's Funeral Home to get your aunt's things. This investigation will go nowhere until we figure out what's in the files these men want."

She nodded. Fifteen minutes later Jasper pulled into the Whisper Mountain Tunnel parking lot. Since he wasn't officially on duty, he'd driven his Jeep. The lot sat empty, a grim warning sign stabbed into the earth, shooing visitors away.

He checked the park ranger lot at the far end of the visitor lot. Noah, a park ranger, was working five miles north, supervising a boat ramp and dock reconstruction in a recreation area. Jasper had texted Noah to let him know they'd be rechecking the tunnel area, to see if he wanted to come by. His brother had answered that he'd let him know if he could join up, but it was unlikely.

They unloaded, Dash launching out with his tail high. Jasper eyed their surroundings as they took off into the woods—the same way he'd gone the night he found Kinsley. She remained silent, inspecting the earth.

The peaceful feeling he always experienced in the woods was long gone.

A raven cawed from the trees then flew to another tree, following them.

"Oh, look at him. What a handsome fella." She cupped a hand to her brow, smiling up at the shiny ebony bird, then glanced Jasper's way. "Did you know a group of ravens is called a conspiracy?"

"I did not know that. Sounds about right."

"They're very intelligent and can imitate sounds like parrots."

He immediately pictured Elsa Tuttle's belligerent macaw, Sunshine. "Too bad that one can't imitate your attacker's voice."

"Yeah." Her chin wedged into her chest, and a sour taste covered his tongue. He should've kept his big mouth closed.

"You look for the device, and I'll keep an eye out for company." He added, "Okay?" To soften his command.

"Got it." Her eyes remained downcast, face aimed at the dirt.

Kinsley zigzagged along the path beside him. At times, she folded into a squat, flicking at the stones and ferns littering the ground. They passed the creek where he'd found her, but nothing shiny glinted under their perusal. When they neared the tunnel, he stopped and whistled for Dash. The Dutch shepherd popped out of a bramble hedge nearby, his posture relaxed and tongue lolling. Still, Jasper's palm rested on his Glock as they approached the tourist site.

Bright yellow tape strung across the opening of tunnel, and overgrown bushes taller than him framed both sides like leafy gates. Another warning sign pierced the earth:

"No Trespassing. Police Investigation Ongoing."

He glanced her way, taking in her shaky posture and rounded eyes. "Sure you're up for this?"

"Yes." The single word wavered like a leaf in the wind. "This is where I was standing when I first heard the man's voice."

He rubbed a damp palm on his shirt. "I really didn't want you to have to relive this."

"I'm not as scared as I thought I'd be. I'm sure because you're here with me."

His chest warmed at her words.

"I just can't believe I forgot about the recorder."

"It was a traumatic experience. Victims often forget details—plus, you have the head wound." Jasper fisted one hand. Just like his. He glared at the tunnel. "Let's take a look inside. Then we'll go over the trail once more and head out. I want to get to the funeral home ASAP."

He was concerned that someone could've tapped her cell. Heard Kinsley's conversation last night. He'd considered contacting Frank Anderson himself but decided against it. It seemed better if only McCoy and law enforcement knew where this file was. At least the law files from the Millers' house were now safely in police custody.

Adrenaline buzzed his temples as they started forward. The more he considered it, the more he felt he should've gone to the funeral home first, open or not. Maybe this jaunt to the tunnel wouldn't have been necessary then. But they were here now. Might as well make the most of the quick visit.

Kinsley grabbed on to the crumbling stone of the tunnel opening, her thoughts mushrooming. She adjusted the small backpack purse she'd brought along.

Was she foolish to come back here while the investigation was still ongoing? Had she dragged Jasper in the wrong direction—should they have gone to the funeral home first? She bent in half, scouring the ground. Nothing so far.

She'd better make this worth their while, then. Find the recorder. Get out of here.

They slipped inside the tunnel, passing the spot where she'd waited when her attacker first approached her. She bumped Jasper's arm as shadows swallowed them whole. If he noticed—or minded—her clumsiness, he didn't show it.

Jasper cleared his throat. "Any thoughts about what this file from your aunt might contain?"

"I've had *lots* of thoughts about it, but I still have no idea. I can't believe Rhonda was involved in anything criminal." It was like believing a hummingbird could take down a hawk.

"I hear you. I don't believe that, either." He hesitated. "Could she know something bad about *you*?"

"Me? I'm not perfect, Jasper, but I don't have any skeletons in my closet." She huffed, then considered his position. Police officer in the midst of an investigation. Asking questions. That was it. "The only person who might have something against me is Marta. My co-worker at the zoo? You checked her out, though, right?"

"I did. The message came through earlier. She was clean," he acknowledged.

"I have been trying to figure out *why* she would do this. It seems way out of character, even for her. I considered texting her to say hi and see how she responds."

"What's Marta like? Is she a levelheaded or emotional person?"

Kinsley pursed her lips. "I guess Marta is kind of up and down with her emotions, but her husband left. She has teenaged kids, and it's been a rough few years."

"Yeah. Single parenthood is the hardest thing I've ever done."

"From what I've seen, you're an amazing dad to Gabe."

"My mom gets a lot of the credit. So do Noah and Brielle, my sister. I don't know where I'd be without my family." He leaned in, picking at a clump of moss on the wall over her head. Their faces were only inches apart. "For now, let law enforcement take care of the situation with Marta. Don't text or call her. Please."

"Okay." Her heart leapfrogged from his nearness.

He inched backward, giving her breathing room. "We'll get this solved. You can attend Rhonda's memorial, then get back home and continue doing what you love."

Her throat convulsed in a swallow. "Thank you."

"There's something else." He paused, looked away. "When I get back to the station later, I'm pulling the files from your parents' accident."

She stiffened. "Why?"

"Because it's my job, and I'm curious. I'm considering all possibilities here. What if there's something about that investigation that—"

"Please don't, Jasper."

"Every time your parents' accident comes up, you shut down."

"You have no room to talk. I used to ask about your dad, but you would clam right up."

He released a drawn-out sigh, and his mouth opened.

Dash growled softly, interrupting what he'd been about to say. Jasper pressed his lips together and held up a hand. The dog's muzzle lifted, and his keen gaze was glued to the woods across from the tunnel. The air rattled in her chest. Had someone followed them?

"Let's move out of sight. Could just be Noah." Jasper clasped her arm and inched back, farther into the darkness. "Could be someone tailing us."

"Would Dash growl at Noah?"

"No," he admitted, "but if he can't get a good scent yet and he hears movement, he'll alert me."

"Let's hope it's Noah, then."

Jasper didn't answer, tugging out his cell instead and texting rapidly. He shoved it back into his pocket, and they continued backing deeper into the tunnel. They were at least ten feet inside now, and the potent smell of moss and mold overtook her senses. Dash whined softly, staring at the entrance.

A skitter of goose bumps covered her arms and legs as he pulled her along. The temperature dropped, and light faded so she could barely see her own hand.

"Did you text Noah?"

"I did, but he hasn't answered yet." Fabric swished, like he was grabbing something from his pocket. Checking his cell. "I don't think we get great reception in here. Let's give it a few minutes, until Dash gives the all clear."

"Okay." She glanced above, but it was impossible to see the stony, bumpy tunnel ceiling. They went around the historical society barrier set up for tourists. Kinsley had never been past it.

Five steps later, he whispered in her ear, "Do you feel that? There's some kind of indent in the wall." He clasped her hand and slid it along the cold, craggy surface. "Here."

She felt a break in the wall; then her fingers skated across a flat, hard surface. She stifled a gasp and pulled back. Was that wood?

She released the oxygen through pinched lips. "That feels like a door." All these years visiting this tunnel with her dad, and there'd been a door back here? Leading to what? An exit outside?

"Jasper?"

Dead silence.

"Jasper!" She turned to set both her palms on the smooth, unexpected surface again but felt only cold air. Her momentum sent her flying through what felt like a black hole, a surprised cry pummeling her throat as she fell forward.

# NINE

Kinsley screamed as two large hands caught her, pulling her headfirst into the dark void. She flailed until the solid wall of Jasper's chest cradled her, his arms wrapping her like an owlet nestled inside its mother's wings. Her backpack purse lay crushed between them, and inky blackness smothered the entire world.

"Jasper?"

"It's okay. I'm here," he whispered.

A solid, furry shape brushed against her knee. *Dash.* Jasper released her, and she mimicked his hushed tone. "Where are we? What is this?"

"That was a door. It's closed now. We're in some kind of room." A tiny light illuminated his face, David against the Goliath-like darkness. His cell.

She grimaced. "I left my phone in your car." She'd been so focused on finding the recorder she forgot her cell.

"This'll have to do. Too bad I don't have my flashlight."

It sounded like he was walking around slowly.

"How did *you* not know about this, Mr. Tunnel Creek Tupperware-Gifter?"

He let out a chuckle from a few feet away. "Maybe

the historical society didn't tell anyone because people will do what we're doing."

The light bobbed farther away from her in the pitch-dark space. Panic welled up inside. "Where are you going?"

"Testing to see how deep this chamber goes."

"Jasper, what if someone else knows about this?" *Like the guys who are after me? Or the person—or people—who set off Dash's canine alarm moments ago?*

He didn't answer. Instead, the *squish* and scuff of his shoes on the damp stone floor resonated through the hidden room. Who was out there in the woods? They hadn't seen anyone, but Jasper seemed confident Dash had sensed a person approaching.

"Who else do you think is out there?"

He moved through the darkness, a disembodied voice. "Might be a ranger checking the area, making sure no one is here. Could be Noah, but I don't think he'd make it back here. Or…"

A dripping sound interrupted their back-and-forth. No, that was faint splashing.

"Or…?" she prompted.

Dash's nails clicked on the ground, and Jasper grunted, scuffling backward quickly. "Dash, no. Leave it."

Kinsley's nails jabbed her palms. "What is it?"

"Rats," Jasper muttered. "Yuck." He returned to her side, the dim cell light flickering across the door. "You okay?"

"Because of the rats? I spent a month during graduate school researching rat populations in urban areas. I'm not scared of rats."

"Well, good for you," he shot back. "What if I am?"

"You don't need to be. It's a rodent that likely weighs

less than one pound and might live a year or two, if he or she is very careful."

"I just don't like them."

"Ah, a phobia, then? That's very normal."

"Maybe. Something bad happened when I lived in… When I was younger. Having one crawl all over you in your bed is not on my highly recommended list of fun activities. Trust me."

"No, I wouldn't like that, either. I'm sorry. I shouldn't have said that." She tilted her head, picturing what he said. "You had a rat crawl over you?"

"You could say that."

Curiosity got a hold of her tongue, and she lowered her voice back to a whisper. "What does that mean?"

"It was a cane rat."

She jerked back. "What? Where were you?" As far as she knew, cane rats only lived in Africa.

"Cameroon." His body went completely still. "We lived there when I was a kid."

*Cameroon?* Shock took over her brain. "What were you doing there?"

"My parents were missionaries. Dad taught English and bible, and Mom used art to connect to the kids. It was a cool experience, living there, until my dad was stranded on a cross-country trip by one of the other people who worked at the hostel." He released a heavy sigh. "The man didn't mean to leave Dad behind—he just got scared, my mom said. But it didn't matter. Dad got lost. Locals searched for days, and they finally found him two weeks later."

Silence echoed between them for several heartbeats.

"Jasper? Was he…?"

"He was gone."

*That's* what had happened to his dad? Her throat

thickened. How could a person hold on to their faith after such a heartbreaking situation? "I'm so sorry."

"Yeah. It was rough. Then we came back stateside, and Mom poured herself into her art to support us."

He was a missionary kid who'd suffered a huge loss. A tentative thread connected them. His loss and hers, tying them together. Shared grief.

She reached out, brushing his forearm. "Jasper—"

"Shh. Don't move," he whispered. "Dash just let me know someone is close by."

Jasper strained to listen. Dash had pressed his muzzle into his thigh twice, then sat and whined. *A warning.*

He flexed his fingers over his weapon. After that admission to Kinsley about his childhood and his dad's death, it felt like his heart was split open and every emotion revealed.

But there was no time to think about that.

His mind shifted gears as the person closed in. The footsteps slowed, and Kinsley's cold fingers gripped his arm. The static of a radio crackled. Jasper didn't recognize the voice—but then again, he could barely hear it.

He closed his eyes, focusing his hearing. More static. Then the voice faded along with the steps. Dash continued sitting, his muscles quivering. If Jasper wasn't mistaken, the man had walked past the door, then turned and headed back out the tunnel.

Kinsley wandered away as he continued listening. They needed to wait a few minutes until it was safe to exit the hidden room. He could barely wait to tell Noah about this. Even though they were oh-for-one as far as the recording device, discovering this space almost made up for it. Did any of the park rangers know about this?

"Jasper, come here. Come feel this," she whispered from several yards away.

He crossed the room carefully. "What is it?"

She was stooped like she was sitting. "There are boxes here. Oh! More."

He turned, searching in the dark, running his hands carefully over what she'd bumped into. Smooth wood containers, inlet handles. At least four feet long. He shuffled sideways, gently pushing her farther down the length of the box so he stood directly in front of it.

*Them.* Make that at least *two* boxes.

He tucked his weapon in his holster, then slipped a finger under the inlet handle on both ends of the lid and lifted. It creaked, and he held it in place until his muscles protested. Then he pulled at it again. The wood was heavier than he'd anticipated. He jerked the lid up and shoved the other hand inside.

His jaw dropped as he felt the contents. Guns. Dozens of them. A few dozen, considering the box's size. The other container was taller and deep. Likely handguns, then. He replaced the lid slowly and stepped back.

His jaw ticked. "These aren't supposed to be here."

"You think they're illegal?"

"Legal operations aren't hidden. Stashed away in the dark like this." Though he wasn't certain, it was a safe guess at this point.

He thumbed through his cell for his camera and snapped pictures. Evidence.

What if—

Could these weapons be related to Willard Tuttle's murder and his attack that day? What if he and Willard had been caught in the middle of something and posed a threat? Had he and the old ranger stumbled upon a gun-trafficking ring—and set off the people selling these?

Illegal weapons were a bigger problem than many people realized. States with weak gun laws often smuggled guns into states with stronger gun laws—and made a ton of money doing it. Enough to kill for, maybe…

They left the boxes the way they found them and waited until Jasper felt it was safe to exit the room.

"Stay here. I'm going to see if we still have company."

Kinsley let out a wobbly breath. "Okay. Just don't leave me here, please."

"I won't."

Jasper felt along the wall as he made his way toward the door. His boot bumped a small object, and it squeaked. He cringed. He'd had nightmares about that cane rat for years. The size of a large cat, it'd gotten through his bedroom window in their small house in Cameroon and tried to get all snuggly under Jasper's blanket. It was the only time in his life he'd screamed. Granted, he was seven.

Jasper continued forward. At the door, he held still and listened for several seconds. No sounds except the occasional gust of wind moaning through the tunnel.

He drew open the door, Dash pushing eagerly against his leg. Darkness spilled out into the tunnel, but no figure met him. He peered toward its mouth, where it gaped wide, letting in a band of sunlight. Jasper looked the other way, to his left. The hidden door sat a few feet past the tourist barrier. No wonder its existence wasn't general knowledge; it blended into the wall.

He stuck his head back in the room. "We're all clear."

They ventured toward the tunnel's entrance. Jasper kept Kinsley behind him as his eyes roved the tree line and the woods beyond the path. His jaw ticked. The creek where he'd found her lay a hundred yards away through the forest.

He pulled out his cell and looked at the screen. "Noah says he's at a recreation site almost an hour away. That wasn't him."

He asked Dash to do an immediate perimeter check while they waited several feet inside. The dog returned with his ears and tail high. All clear. Whoever had been here had gotten far enough away that they weren't in Dash's crosshairs.

"Straight back to the parking lot. You keep checking for the recording device, but continue moving forward. Stay close."

"Okay."

With his eyes on their surroundings and one hand on his weapon, they retraced their earlier steps. Kinsley stalled at several spots, lifting branches and toeing aside dead limbs. Her posture was slumped by the time they hit the parking lot. Still no device.

Ten feet from the Jeep, Jasper's heart *thunked* into his boots.

"No!" He rushed forward. Kinsley followed. His front tires were slashed, and the Jeep's soft-cover top ripped open. Someone had rummaged through his vehicle.

He examined the damage, then checked the leather-and-plastic top. Who had done this? There were no cars in the area. Strange. Had their follower been on foot? Jasper tugged out his phone to take a picture of the man-made slashes.

Dash let out a warning bark a couple seconds before the *ping, ping* of bullets rent the air. Jasper grabbed Kinsley and tucked her to his chest as he launched sideways on the pavement beside the Jeep. Pain spider-webbed across his ribs at the impact. Where were the shots coming from? He whistled sharply. Dash moved to his side with the canine scramble he'd been trained to use during gunfire.

"Where do we go?" Kinsley cried. "Can we get inside your car?"

It'd be a death trap if the person came closer. "No. Hold still." At least from here, they had the option to run if needed. Where was the shooter positioned? He craned his neck to catch all the possible angles.

An older-model silver sedan crashed out from between a small storage unit and a thick stand of trees. The squeal of speeding tires on pavement ignited Jasper's nerves. Branches cracked and leaves littered the air as the car sped across the parking lot toward the exit road. The perp had been hiding at the edge of the woods. Jasper sat up, aimed his weapon and shot off two rounds. The bullets *dinged* into the trunk of the departing car, missing the wheels by inches.

Kinsley tucked into a ball at the loud noise and recoil.

The silver car flew down the exit, disappearing through the trees. No wonder he couldn't get a license number—there wasn't one.

Jasper tugged out his cell, then growled. The screen was crushed. He pressed the face of the phone, but it didn't respond, showing only the gray reflection of his face fractured into a hundred pieces.

"Great. My phone is toast." When he dove to the ground, the phone must've caught the brunt of his weight.

"Looks that way." The rumble of the engine vanished from earshot. Dash sat up, brown eyes pinned on Jasper. He wasn't positive, but that car appeared to be the same one from the night of Kinsley's first attack.

"The person hid behind the storage unit." How the

car had fit, Jasper wasn't sure. "Let's see if they left your phone. Otherwise…"

"Otherwise, we have no way to communicate with anyone." She sat up.

"Exactly." If only the cameras on the ranger cabin worked. The day of their attack, Willard mentioned the cameras hadn't been working at the Whisper Mountain Tunnel for a while. Three, four months? Two cameras had been found busted, he'd told Jasper, and the rangers hadn't fixed them yet.

*Willard Tuttle.* The hair on his arms stood up, and questions tangled in his mind like ropes. What if all this was tied together—Willard Tuttle's murder and Jasper's head injury, Kinsley's attacks, Rhonda Miller's death, and now the guns? Did the person who'd just shot at them know what they'd discovered—and was the shooter involved in the likely illegal gun trafficking?

He blinked, his focus returning to their current predicament. Walking along the main road was a risk, and they'd be at the mercy of any car driving past. An idea formed. Jasper hurriedly checked the Jeep. Kinsley's phone was MIA, as expected, and his radio was broken. He motioned for Kinsley to follow him to the side of the ranger station. The main door was locked, but at least they were out of sight.

He jammed his busted cell into his pocket. "You up for a short hike?"

She wiped dirt and grit from the ground off of her shirt. "Sure. Where to? Your cabin?"

"Not mine. There's a friend closer. And she has a spare vehicle."

Kinsley's eyes mapped his face like she was checking to see if he was joking. "What if this friend doesn't want to see you on such short notice?"

"She will." He whistled at Dash. "I got a better description of the car from the night you were attacked. I need to call that in at her house." He looked around before stepping out from behind the ranger station. "Let's get going."

She followed, her brow crinkled. Wondering where they were going, no doubt.

He needed to call in what had happened and find them a ride, then get to the funeral home ASAP. Jasper had two strong premonitions about this case after their find in the tunnel.

One, the answers they needed were in that file of her aunt's; and two, the men after them were no longer attempting to kidnap Kinsley.

Now they wanted her dead.

Kinsley kept her eyes glued to Jasper's back as they entered the tree line. Questions buzzed like mosquitoes through her mind, but she kept returning to what had just happened. Sweat dampened the back of her shirt from the frightening encounter in the parking lot. Once again, Jasper had protected her. And he'd been right—they shouldn't have come here. Yet he'd never gotten angry or blamed her for any of this. Through all of it, Jasper remained a kind, steady person. Even his bossiness originated from his caretaker's heart.

She mashed her lips together, shaking the thoughts away.

"Dash, check perimeter."

The dog loped forward, tail high, racing ahead as they hiked. The bright chirps of cardinals and the raucous cries of blue jays filled her ears, a welcome chorus of wildlife that momentarily pushed away her fear. The song of her heart from a young age.

Still, the pleasant harmony couldn't erase what had just happened—how close they'd come to getting shot.

Dash returned, his tongue flopping and eyes trained on Jasper. He circled Jasper, then sat.

"We're safe. The shooter must've been alone. Let's keep moving."

She trotted to keep up with Jasper's long strides. "How far away is this friend of yours?"

"About a mile." Mud slurped beneath his shoes. "She lives on the other side of Whisper Mountain. My cabin is further away, and we'd have to take roads to get there."

Kinsley's eyes narrowed at his vagueness.

They hiked for several minutes, with quiet floating between them. Kinsley tried to take in the forest, their surroundings. Sumter National Forest was beautiful this time of year. Lush. Green. Humming with life. But she was hard-pressed to enjoy God's creation with so much fear and uncertainty stalking her.

*Thou wilt keep him in perfect peace, whose mind is stayed on thee: because he trusteth in thee.*

Peace. How in the world could she find that when men were shooting at her?

They approached a crumbling stone wall. Dash cleared it easily, then Jasper. He reached across and offered her a hand. She set her hand firmly in his, then clambered over the wall, landing atop a blackberry bramble. Berries splattered and thorns pricked her shins. The deep purple liquid oozed like…

*Blood.* She looked up at him, pictured the blood on the side of his face last night. Considered how close they'd come to dying in the old glass warehouse. Kinsley dragged in a breath. She'd brought Jasper heartache a decade ago, and her current situation added more stress and danger to his life. She touched the bandage on her forehead. Now he had one, too. Her heart turned over. She didn't understand why all this was happening, but she did know that Jasper would be much better off when this case was solved and she was gone from his life.

He half lifted her across the thorny bush she'd landed on. "Is your head hurting?"

She slipped her hand from his and shook her head. Warmth climbed her neck at his scrutiny.

"We're almost there." He turned, trudging onward. A few minutes later, they emerged from the woods and into a clearing.

A cozy one-story house grabbed her attention. Not too big, not too small, the white clapboard home had blue shutters and was situated beside a two-story garage. Dash took off across the well-kept yard just as a dachshund trilled a welcome on the front porch. The dogs rendezvoused like old buddies, their tails wagging a mile a minute. Behind the porch railing, an elderly woman sat in a rocking chair. Kinsley's eyes rounded. Was that a *bird* perched on a stand beside her? An ear-splitting cawing filled the air, either a welcome or a warning.

Yes. A macaw. *Incredible.*

Kinsley hesitated as Jasper trotted toward the house. Who lived here, and was she trustworthy? Because right now, it felt like Jasper was the only person in the world she could rely on.

# TEN

Jasper waited until Mrs. Elsa Tuttle stepped far away from Sunshine's huge bird stand before wrapping the petite woman in a gentle embrace. One of his eyes remained on the feathered menace. She stood on the main level of the porch, while he planted himself two steps down. In the safety zone.

"It's good to see you again," he said. "Everything okay at your place?"

"Yes, dear." Her warm smile slipped. "But you look like something the cat dragged in." Mrs. Tuttle's forehead wrinkled up like an accordion. "Did something happen?"

"You could say that." He really couldn't share about the case. "It's been a rough morning, but we're okay. And we won't stay long." He twisted around to see if Kinsley had followed. "I brought company."

"Wonderful. I love company."

Kinsley stopped in the front yard to pet Thunder. The gold-colored dachshund vetted the new human, demanding back-scratching before wiggling over to lay beside Dash. His canine partner tucked into his favorite cool dirt spot beneath the boxwoods at the front of the house.

Jasper turned back to Mrs. Tuttle. "I have a favor to ask."

"Let me guess. You want more of my key lime pie? I'm sorry, son, but that pie is long gone." She cooed at Sunshine. The gigantic bird bobbed his bright red head.

"All mine, mine," Sunshine said in jarring, near-perfect English. Jasper shuddered.

He scowled at the bird, then addressed Mrs. Tuttle. "You know I love your pies, but what I need is to borrow the Corolla." He grimaced. As old as the vehicle was, it worked.

The steps shook as Kinsley came up beside him. "Hello. What a beautiful macaw."

"Why, thank you." Mrs. Tuttle tilted her head. "And you are Kinsley Miller, right? How you've grown up. Such a lovely young woman." She sent Jasper a raised-brow look—which he ignored—before addressing Kinsley again. "I'm very sorry about your aunt. Rhonda was a dear woman. To lose my Willard and Rhonda in a few weeks' time..." She sighed.

A fleeting wounded expression crossed Kinsley's face. "Thank you. I'm sorry for your loss, too." Kinsley tilted her head, staring at the older woman. "Wait, are you the Mrs. Tuttle from middle school?"

Jasper gave her credit for remembering. Mrs. Tuttle had taught sixth and seventh grade English at Tunnel Creek Middle for many years before retiring.

"Yes, dear, that's me." Mrs. Tuttle's keen brown eyes jumped from Kinsley to Jasper. "Did you say you need my *car*?"

"Yes, ma'am. My Jeep's out of commission. We, ah, need to get back to town as soon as possible." He left it at that, and her eyebrows shot up. Mrs. Tuttle didn't miss anything.

"You're welcome to the Corolla. That's why Willard and I kept it around. Why don't you come inside for something to drink first?"

Ten minutes later they'd downed a couple of Arnold Palmers each and filled up on the apple-crumb-cake muffins Mrs. Tuttle had baked that morning. Dash begged off a handful of bone-shaped dog treats and settled in a curled-up position on the living room rug.

Jasper had also used the older woman's home phone to call Dispatch and relay what had happened in the Whisper Mountain Tunnel parking lot. An APB was out for the silver car. Jasper checked the time; they needed to get on the road.

Mrs. Tuttle read his mind. "I imagine you want to leave soon."

He gave her a nod, and she headed toward her bedroom to retrieve her car keys. Her slippers rustled against the wood floors Jasper and Willard had installed last year.

Kinsley waited until she was in the room, then whispered, "Are we putting her in danger being here?"

"Do you see that bird? *We're* the ones in danger." He glared toward the corner of the kitchen, where Sunshine's large green metal cage was parked next to a window. The blinds were opened, and sunlight streamed over the large creature Mrs. Tuttle had carried in when they'd come inside. "I don't get the name."

"Sunshine seems harmless to me." She gazed adoringly at the bird, and he slapped his drink on the counter. *Harmless?*

"Here they are." Mrs. Tuttle shuffled back into the room, holding a silver key ring with a small blue-and-gold parrot key chain. "You'll be filling my tank up as well, hmm?"

"Of course we will." He smiled, nabbing the keys with a "Thank you" and a peck on the older woman's gray head.

Kinsley pushed off the counter and took a couple of tentative steps toward the bird.

Just making eye contact with Sunshine gave him the heebie-jeebies. "Don't you need all your fingers for your work?"

"Would you like to feed Sunshine?" Elsa wobbled over to Kinsley.

"Only if you think he wouldn't mind." Kinsley edged closer, and the macaw climbed down from its highest perch. Watching. Moving closer to Kinsley.

"If you have a treat, he'll become your best friend." Mrs. Tuttle retrieved a small bag of bird food on a rack below the cage. She withdrew an almond and handed it to Kinsley.

Jasper crossed his arms. Why was he so worried? Kinsley was a biologist. She'd probably been bitten by all sorts of animals. Definitely by lizards. Rats? Maybe even coyotes. He could do nothing here but warn her. "We have to get going."

She looked over her shoulder at him, her face a maze of emotions. Eagerness, caution and joy. She loved animals. Always had. She'd once yelled at another student for trying to kill a wolf spider in homeroom before she found a container to catch it and release it outside.

But there was no stopping her once her mind was made up.

"I'll wait outside. Two minutes." He couldn't watch.

Jasper cut through the kitchen and headed back out the entryway.

They needed to get to the funeral home first thing. Secure her aunt's things, then bring them in as evidence. Figure out what was inside it that warranted all these attacks.

He strode past Willard Tuttle's F-150, then opened the garage slash workshop door. The Tuttle's spare car sat inside, looking like a kid's toy on steroids. The paint was bleached on the roof despite spending many of its days inside the man shed. It would work for today. Jasper held his breath and started the Corolla. The engine sputtered twice, then turned over, and he backed the vehicle out into the driveway.

Just in time to witness Kinsley stepping out of the front door, a feathered blob of red death on her shoulder.

He threw it in Park, climbed out, and whistled for Dash. His partner trotted over and jumped in.

Kinsley held still, an enchanted expression on her face. What was she feeding that thing?

"He likes pineapple," she called out.

Then he should be on a tropical island in the Caribbean. "We need to get going."

Sunshine squawked, one beady eye fixed on him, then fluffed his feathers so full he looked half the size of Kinsley. Twice the size he should be.

Kinsley set her shoulder next to Mrs. Tuttle's. "Step down, Sunshine."

"I love you."

Jasper cocked his head. "Did that bird just say, 'I love you'?"

Elsa Tuttle chuckled softly as she shoulder-carried the bird to his perch on the porch. "Sunshine has taken to Ms. Miller the way you did to Kinsley in high school, Jasper."

Heat climbed his neck, but he waved a dismissive hand.

Kinsley finally joined him, her hair falling around

her shoulders. He dragged his gaze to the rustic interior of the car. She looked too good for a person who'd been attacked multiple times over the last three days.

They waved goodbye, then headed down the driveway. After riding in his Jeep, the Corolla made it feel like they were sitting right on the road.

"That was fun." Kinsley held out something bright red. "Look, Mrs. Tuttle gave me a souvenir feather. Isn't it beautiful?"

He snorted. "You are in the right field. No doubt about it."

Jasper pulled out onto Whisper Mountain Road. Clouds gathered overhead, and the forest closed in around them, cutting off the sunlight.

She set the feather on the dashboard. "It's unfortunate that she lives out there by herself."

"It's only four miles from town. But yeah, I know. Feels remote. I wish she'd sell and move closer. She said she's not ready yet."

"Did you know her husband well?"

"We had worked together before. He is—was—a park ranger." Jasper strangled the steering wheel between his palms. "Noah worked with him more than I did. But he was like a second father to us. My head injury happened at the same time Willard was killed." *He's dead because of me*, Jasper didn't say. "There's a lot about that day that gives me nightmares. Like how I should've figured out it was an ambush." His tongue stuck to the roof of his mouth. "Willard would still be alive if I'd been more alert."

"You blame yourself for his death?"

"How can I not?"

Silence settled inside the car. It was easy to talk to

Kinsley—too easy. He'd already shared too much. What if she questioned his ability to protect her now?

"Mrs. Tuttle sang your praises back there. She said you help with things around the house all the time, and have for years. She doesn't seem the type to hold you responsible for a terrible situation out of your control." Kinsley shifted in her seat. "Where are we going now?"

"I should go to the station. But first we're going to the funeral home. Once we do, I need to spend a couple hours at the station." Checking all the files, writing reports. Pulling mug shots. Filling in McCoy.

The winding road narrowed, the steep, ascending hill on the passenger side making it one lane. Another reason he didn't want Mrs. Tuttle driving into town often.

"When we get to the funeral home, I'll— Whoa, what's that?"

Movement caught his eye on Kinsley's side of the road. Up ahead, rocks tumbled down the hill, smashing into one another. Dirt and grass kicked up as the car drew closer. A rockslide?

Kinsley shrieked as a suitcase-sized boulder plowed into the passenger side of the Corolla. He jerked the steering wheel left. It hadn't rained yet, so what had started the slide? A stone the size of his fist smacked into the windshield, cracking the glass as it bounced off. Dash let out a sharp, alerting bark. Then another.

Jasper's pulse exploded. Someone was nearby. The dog had seen something.

"Hang on!" He slammed on the brakes, weaving around the rocks. On the other side of the road, a steep incline continued the drop. In a split second, both choices flashed through his mind: either drive through the maze of rocks and hope they make it or veer sharp left and take the loaner car on a nosedive into a ditch.

A jagged gray boulder rumbled toward them, forcing his decision. Jasper floored it, but the rock caught the back end of the vehicle, yanking it left anyway. They crashed into a stand of bushes and small trees before the front end dropped. The tires kicked up gravel and debris as gravity grabbed hold of the Corolla and sent them downward toward the river.

Jasper's eyes snagged on a man standing uphill— where the rockslide had started, dusting his hands off like his job there was finished.

As the car tipped violently down the steep hill, the person disappeared. Leaving Jasper with time for only one thought: *Maybe they were?*

Kinsley slammed against her seat belt as the small vehicle sank forward, the tires spinning and the engine whirring as the trunk rose off the concrete. Dash thumped into the back of her seat, then yelped, trying to gain his footing.

Jasper's arm and the seat belt were all that kept her from cracking her head on the dashboard.

"There's a tree—ooph!" Jasper shouted as the Corolla slid easily over the damp ground, propelled by the boulder's mass. What if they missed the tree and kept going lower? It was the only thing that might stop them. A sliver of shiny blue shimmered far down the ravine, the hill turning steeply into a sure-death drop.

Whoever set off the rockslide had made sure it would happen at this exact spot in the road for this reason.

"Jasper, the river." The air was sucked out of her diaphragm as they slid closer and closer to the huge oak that leaned slightly sideways on the side of the hill. *Please, God, keep us safe.*

"I see it. Pray we stop here!"

"I am!"

The car bumped over a couple of stumps before picking up speed again and roaring toward the tree. Her heart lodged in her throat.

"Brace yourself!" he shouted and leaned toward her, his arm flung across her like a second seat belt. The crunch of metal and the bone-shaking thud of the impact jarred every cell in her body, and she cried out.

Everything froze like they were in a movie and viewers had hit the pause button. Except this was real, and they were in terrible danger. She held her breath for what felt like minutes. Waiting. Wondering…would they keep falling?

An eerie stillness insulated them. Something hissed in the engine. She sent up a prayer of thanks, then set her hands on her seat belt. Beside her, Jasper's head rolled sideways, blood dribbling from his lip.

"Jasper!" She tried to unbuckle her seat belt, but he was sprawled partially over her and the dashboard in the small car. Even in the last moment before wrecking, he'd been thinking of her. Protecting her.

Tears burned her eyes. How would she get him out of here?

"Jasper. Please. Say something." She turned her head to find Dash unscrambling his long legs. The dog let out a low whine. "Are you okay, boy?"

He pushed his muzzle through the headrest, licking her neck, then nudging Jasper. Nothing. He lay as still as…

No. He couldn't be dead. He'd probably sustained a head injury against the dashboard, but he was okay. He had to be. Smoke had begun to curl out from the engine in thin wafts.

"Please, God, help me get him out of here." What could she do?

Kinsley worked her arm through his arm and side, attempting to unbuckle herself. Then she did the same with him. Sunlight broke through the clouds and poured through the fragmented front windshield of the small vehicle tucked against the oak tree.

*Mrs. Tuttle's poor car. And Jasper!* Kinsley cupped his cheek and jawline. Then she lowered her head to make sure he was breathing.

He was! *Thank You, God.*

Through a thick branch, the river sparkling below caught her eyes. Her throat closed. What if moving meant the crushed vehicle dislodged from the tree speed bump and finished the fall down the mountain?

She couldn't leave him. There had to be a way to get him out of the car.

Jasper moaned, his head bumping into her shoulder.

"Shh. Hang on. I'm here." She closed her eyes and whispered another prayer: "Please, God, help me get him out of here in time."

Smoke was billowing now, the acrid smell burning her nose.

She wiggled toward her door, her right hand searching for the handle. It worked, but the door wouldn't open. A quick inspection of the window showed a thick, lower branch wedged against the door. She turned the manual window crank, but it dropped an inch, then stuck. Wouldn't go back up, wouldn't go down.

Dash whined in the back seat, trying to push through onto the console.

"I know, boy. Stay still. Hold." What was the word he'd use to keep the dog from moving? "I'm working on getting us out of here."

She was thankful Jasper had already reclined his seat quite a bit because of his large frame and long legs. She pivoted in the seat, tugged the headrest out and then stabbed the glass with the metal spikes. The damaged glass shuddered, then gave way. Pieces of glass littered her hair and lap.

Pushing the rest of the broken pieces out of the window, Kinsley shoved her arms and upper body through the opening, careful not to trip on the limb propped against the door. A sizzle of pain burned her thigh, but she ignored it and launched herself, landing with a hard thud. She sprawled across the ground to keep herself from flying downhill.

She stood, her legs wobbly like a fawn's, and opened the back-passenger door. Dash climbed out, then bumped his nose into her open palm. What did that mean? The dog turned and leaped right back into the vehicle, pressing his muzzle under Jasper's left arm.

He groaned softly.

Her chest warmed at the display of loyalty. "I'm not leaving him, either, boy. But we need to figure out how to get him out of the car without hurting him or moving it anymore."

She rounded the back of the vehicle, which was leaning against the steep incline, and surveyed the damage. The car was clearly totaled, its front end crumpled, front-left tire bent from impact with the oak tree. Smoke curled from the engine. Sticks and leaves dotted the hood and roof, and the front door was creased near where it connected to the front end. Would Jasper's door even open?

She swiped her hair from her face and tried. Slowly. Carefully.

Nothing. The doorframe was jammed hard and

wouldn't budge. Continuing to try risked rocking the car. She opened the back driver-side door, whistling for Dash. The dog gazed at her with his intelligent brown eyes, emitted an unhappy woof and jumped out, worrying the ground along the driver side of the vehicle.

Kinsley climbed into the back seat and gently cradled Jasper's head. He startled slightly as her cool hands pressed around his cheeks. "Jasper, can you hear me?"

The car wobbled and groaned in its precarious position against the massive oak tree. Her heart rate picked up. Between the smoke and the drop, the odds weren't looking good.

"Jasper," she said, raising her voice. "We have to get you out of here. Please."

Adrenaline burned her veins. Could she drag him out through the back door? Kinsley reached to the side of his seat, working on the reclining handle. It was old and stuck. She tried again, her knuckles turning white as she pushed it up with all her strength.

There! It gave way, lifting, and she used her other arm to push his seat lower. As low as it would go, so his head and upper body lay practically across the back seat—and Kinsley's lap. Thank the Lord for the small interior. Jasper was already practically in the back seat.

But how to get him out?

The car creaked again as though irritated with all the movement. Then the frame shuddered, dipping left—not the way she wanted the vehicle to go.

What if...? She grabbed her small backpack and looped one thin strap through his left arm. Would this hurt him? What if he had a neck injury? Kinsley looped both arms around him and clenched her hands. She had to take the risk to get him out of this car. Her intuition told her time was running out. The damp ground would eliminate traction for the tires, and in minutes—seconds?—the little Corolla could careen down the incline, into the rocky river bottom below.

*God, I need strength. Wake him up, please.*

Kinsley whistled at Dash. "Here, boy. Grab this." She detached the other strap of her backpack, prayed the straps would hold and then motioned for the dog to grasp it with his teeth. Dash mouthed it for a moment, then dropped it and sat on his haunches.

"Come on, boy. You have to do this." Did Jasper use certain words with the dog? Command words? "Grab. Hold." The dog sniffed the strap, then mouthed it again, finally grasping it with his sharp white teeth.

"Good boy! That's it. Hold. Okay, hold." The space was so tight, with Jasper right outside the back driver-side door and Kinsley crouched on the back seat, it was difficult to maneuver so that they would both be pulling in the same direction.

She knelt, positioning herself so she could turn to her left to tug him out of the vehicle.

"Okay. Here we go."

Kinsley looped her arms around Jasper's right arm and tugged. "Dash, let's pretend he's a bear. A big bear we just drugged to tag and check its vitals."

The dog cocked his head, and Jasper muttered something she couldn't make out. Overhead, the sky rumbled out a threat as storms spread across the horizon. Now she was racing against the car's downward projection *and* the weather.

"Ready, pull!" She tugged, pulling up and to the left as Dash yanked from outside the vehicle. Jasper inched toward her, his head nearly to her ribs. There! Could she turn him now?

"Dash, pull!" She pushed his right shoulder as Dash

tugged on the backpack in quick, strong jerks with his powerful mouth and neck muscles. "Good boy! Keep going."

Jasper groaned, thrashing his head back and forth.

"What—where... Kinsley?"

*Thank You, God!* "Jasper! You're awake. I could use a little help here."

Something popped under the car, and it slid forward and to the left. Dash yelped and let go to jump out of the way. The car slid more, and she crab-crawled to stay beside it.

Wind whipped up from the chasm below.

"Jasper! Move!"

He pushed off the seat with a grunt, rolling himself through the back door.

"That's it!" Her muscles burned as she tugged and he scrambled out of and away from the perilous situation. Their momentum sent them a couple of feet outside the car, and the vehicle bounced once Jasper's weight was withdrawn from the interior.

That last movement was all the little car needed. It made a slow, sliding turn and catapulted the rest of the way down the mountainside, landing in a burst of flames on the riverbank before it flipped one more time, extinguishing itself in the water.

Kinsley collapsed to the ground beside Jasper, her chest heaving. A grateful prayer fell from her lips.

"Kins..."

"I'm here." She lay her arm across him as Dash hovered around his master, sniffing and nudging. "Easy, boy. Give him space." She stroked the dog's shoulder.

"Where..."

"Out of the car. On the ground."

His poor battered face couldn't hide his eye roll. "Location?"

She thought back to the short drive from Elsa Tuttle's home on the backside of Whisper Mountain. "Maybe a mile, mile and a half from Mrs. Tuttle's house. I'm not sure. I haven't come this way in so long, and I wasn't paying close attention."

"Near…the river?"

"Yes." Too close for comfort.

A raindrop splattered on her nose, trickled down her cheek. That rockslide hadn't just been conveniently timed. She'd seen a man standing at the top of the hill, holding something. Maybe one of those remote detonators she'd seen in the movies? Dash had barked just before they'd gone over the edge, too, and Kinsley had a feeling he'd been trying to alert them to the person's presence. Was it the same person who'd shot at them in the Whisper Mountain Tunnel lot? Were they being followed?

Her gaze skimmed Jasper's prone form, then lifted to the steep embankment they had to climb to get out of there. Could he make it up the incline? And what if the man was waiting for them at the top, near the road… What could they do?

Because no matter where she turned, it seemed like someone was out to get her.

# ELEVEN

"That rockslide was started on purpose," Jasper huffed as they crawled up the hill. Every few feet he slowed as the world spun. "Dash gave the alerting bark right before we went off the road." And hadn't there been someone standing at the top of the hill?

He wasn't sure, his head throbbed so bad.

"What if the man who shot at us in the parking lot started the landslide?" She swiped dirt off her shorts. Dash sniffed a clump of wildflowers nearby, his watchful gaze following his and Kinsley's slow progress.

"You saw the person on top of that hill next to the road?"

"Yeah, but just a quick look. He moved out of sight."

"Man, what a day." He stretched his shoulders, rolled his head around slowly—all of which was still intact because of Kinsley. "Thanks for pulling me out of that car."

Her back stiffened. "I wouldn't have left you there, Jasper."

"I know that. But I'm not a small guy."

"No, but I'm determined."

"And I'm grateful for that."

They started up the next section of the hill. Five steps

and lots of sweat later, he stopped to rest. Only twenty yards or so to go.

She squinted up at the thick gunmetal-gray clouds spitting light rain down on them, then closed her eyes. "I shouldn't have come back."

"What about your aunt's service?"

"It's not worth all of this. Look at what's happened to you. If I hadn't come back, you'd be playing with Gabriel right now, working or helping your mom. Your life would be just as it was three days ago." She opened her eyes, and her voice wavered. "Now we have matching head wounds. We totaled a sweet older lady's car, damaged a historic grist mill, caused a glass factory to be blown up and put your family in harm's way. I'm starting to think…"

He gritted his jaw as an ache echoed through his skull. "You're starting to think…what?"

"Oh, Jasper! I can tell you're in pain. We need to get you to the hospital." She thrust her shoulder under his arm, and they hobbled side by side to a medium-sized boulder partially buried under the earth. He propped himself against the cold surface, grimacing until the pain passed.

"What were you going to say?" He leaned forward, settling his head in his hands.

From the corner of his half-closed eyes, he noticed her threading her fingers into a tight knot. "I was going to say that it seems like anyone who gets close to me ends up hurt."

"That's not true."

"Yes, it is."

"I don't know what happened to your parents all those years ago, but *it wasn't your fault*. It was an accident." He straightened, rubbing his neck and looking her way. "We'll get to the bottom of what happened to Rhonda. But none of this is your fault."

"It sure feels that way." She met his eyes.

"I get it. I'd probably think along the same lines. You know I feel all messed up about Willard Tuttle."

She sagged closer to him.

He ignored the warning bells ringing in his ears and drew her under his arm. They huddled together in the misting rain, staring out over the green valley below. Kinsley fit like she was made to be right there, and Jasper choked back a contented sigh.

The ache in his head and soreness across his back felt a million miles away.

"What does the Bible say about condemnation?"

"That it ruins your life?"

"Close." He cleared his throat. "I think the Bible says, 'There is therefore now no condemnation to them which are in Christ Jesus.'"

She hummed softly. "There is something extra special about hearing God's word spoken aloud while standing in the middle of His beautiful creation."

"Even without animals in the picture?"

"Well, there is Dash." She pointed to his partner rolling on his back in the grass slightly downhill. They laughed as the dog flopped around, legs wriggling skyward in pure enjoyment.

"Yeah. He's such a beast." Under different circumstances, sitting and laughing with her might've become a favorite memory. But this was temporary. They had to get back into town. Get to the funeral home. He had reports to write after he got his head checked out—again.

He pulled his arm away. "So, no more guilt about your parents. Got it?"

"The same goes for you about Mr. Tuttle. Besides,

what're you going to do, arrest me if I feel bad?" Her teasing smile mesmerized him.

"Maybe I will. Maybe I'll sentence you to Saturdays digging up earthworms for Grandma's garden, with a six-year-old boy who loves critters but whose father does not."

"That sounds fun, actually."

The sound of an approaching vehicle carried down from the road. Kinsley jumped to her feet, then scrambled up the incline. Dash flipped over, shook the grass off and came over to bump his nose into Jasper. Jasper rose and followed Kinsley, growling from how slow he had to move or else the world tilted sideways. *Please, Lord, let this be someone we can trust.*

"Be careful, Kinsley. It could be a—"

"It's a Tunnel Creek Police car!"

He angled his face skyward and whispered, "Thank you."

Two hours later he and Kinsley pulled out of Tunnel Creek General Hospital with Officer Chris Anders, who'd found them roadside. Jasper's throbbing head had been checked thoroughly, and he'd been cleared to go home. The doctor recommended minimal physical activity for the next week, which had gone in one ear and out the other. He'd take it easy once this case was solved. After speaking with the chief, Jasper had called to have his Jeep towed and then contacted Elsa Tuttle. He'd promised to work around her house on any home repair projects as well as mow her lawn indefinitely to cover the loss of the trusty little spare car. Elsa took in the news in stride, asking several times if he, Kinsley, and Dash were okay.

Thank the Lord they *were* all okay. But Jasper didn't park on that point for long because the rockslide insti-

gator and the shooter were still out there. Could it be
the man who'd kidnapped Kinsley and set the bomb?
Or were they one and the same? He shifted his feet in
the squad car. Possible. Everything about this case was
still unsettled. Uncertain.

They needed the items from her aunt. Needed to go
through Kinsley's dad's legal paperwork. Needed to
figure out what these criminals wanted. Unfortunately,
the chief had demanded the reports for today's events
had to be filled out ASAP. Which meant retrieving the
items from the funeral home had to be pushed back another hour or two.

He gazed out the window as Chris drove them to the
station. Kinsley sat in back with Dash. Houses lined the
roadside, people on their porches and children running
through sprinklers. To the right, the huge field that had
once been a farm now housed the Tunnel Creek Drive-
In. Trixie's Ice Cream and Treats sat beside that, the
former barn gone, replaced with a giant ice-cream cone
building. They passed the two-story brick library; then
Marvin's, the favorite gathering place of local teens after
school. Marv had the best burgers. He and Kinsley had
ventured there a few times their senior year for Friday-
night dates. Burgers and malts.

"I should get a strawberry malt before I leave."

"You should." He shifted, turning carefully to catch
Kinsley noticing the same sights and landscape he had.
She glanced forward and caught him looking at her.

He swiveled back around, crushing the seat belt in
his palm.

"Looks like Chief is out for the rest of the day," Chris
said, repeating what Jasper had found out when he'd
spoken with McCoy earlier. "He's at the Elk's Lodge
for the Rotary Club meeting." Chris grumbled under his

breath about not being able to keep up with the chief's schedule. "Sounds like he's been out stumping for Barnhill. Upcoming election, you know?"

"Do you mean the same David Barnhill who ran for mayor the year we graduated?" Kinsley asked. "How can he still run?"

"Same man." Jasper relaxed his hold on the seat belt. "This is a small town. No term limits."

"I heard this'll be his last run. Supposedly, Barnhill wants one of those hot seats in DC next," Chris joked as he entered the station parking lot. "I say good riddance. I'm about done with tax hikes all the time just because we live next to a national forest." The younger officer parked, then winked at Jasper. "But you didn't hear me say that, right?"

"Say what?" Jasper had bigger things to consider than Mayor Barnhill and his plans. He opened the door, and they exited the vehicle, three doors slamming in succession.

Puddles soaked the parking lot. A thunderstorm had doused the area earlier, though thankfully, the heaviest rain had held off until he and Kinsley were inside the hospital.

Chris unlocked the station door, and they entered the quiet building in a single file line, with Dash at Jasper's heel. Once they passed the reception area, Chris broke away for his office.

"Thanks for the ride," Jasper called out. "Let me know what the team finds back at the rockslide."

Chris saluted. "You got it, Holt."

As soon as the other officer disappeared into his office, Kinsley turned to Jasper.

"Did anyone ever pick up the legal paperwork from my dad's office at our house?"

"Done. It's all in Records and Evidence. Right now, I have reports to write about the rock slide and the tunnel. As soon as I'm finished, we'll head over to the funeral home."

She peered down the hall. "Where does Dash go while you're here?"

"During normal business hours, he has to be with me in my office. He's got a crate with a bed in there. But when it's after hours or the weekend, he gets his choice." He ducked his head, dropping his voice to a whisper. "Don't tell anyone, but he likes to go around and sniff the other guy's chairs. I don't even want to know why."

"Neither do I." She grinned back, but the smile couldn't hide the pale purple smudges below her eyes or the sluggish way she moved. She might've gotten medically cleared at the hospital, but this ordeal was taking a major toll on her.

"Do you want to rest in the break room with Dash while I write my reports and start looking through records?"

She nodded. "That sounds good. Unless Officer Anders will need in the break room?"

"I doubt it. He's in his office, making a call. He'll be going back out to look at the rock slide soon. Why don't you go sit down? Grab a snack and a drink, if you want. Chips and protein bars in the cabinet, soda and water in the fridge." He pointed to the largest room in the station, where filing cabinets were lined up, filled with paperwork from the last seven years of Tunnel Creek's not-so-exciting criminal history. Only in the last few years had the tiny police station gone totally electronic.

"My computer is under repair, so I'll be at the workstation in there."

"Okay." She set off, then pivoted in the break room doorway. "I hope you listen to what the doctor said. If you feel dizzy or experience nausea, come in here and tell me. Please."

"Yes, ma'am. And you get some rest."

"Deal."

Jasper retraced his steps to Anders's office to mention the broken cameras at the Whisper Mountain Tunnel lot. He paused outside the door as his coworker's voice carried out. Laughter, then teasing, then a hushed tone. He must be talking to his wife.

Jasper turned around and headed back to Records. His feet felt like they weighed fifty pounds each. Kinsley had gently plied him with a request to tell her if he didn't feel well moments ago. Instead of bothering him, her petition had felt like an invisible hug—like she cared enough to bug him. Which he was only used to from Mom. And sometimes Noah and Brielle.

An ache dug under his ribs. What would that be like, to have a girlfriend or wife checking on him? Thinking about him? Someone to laugh with, share meals with and raise a family beside. Grow together in their faith, too. He and Michelle had never been a cohesive team, even though he'd tried to make her happy.

He shook off the memories and questions. No sense in going there. The Records and Evidence door creaked when he opened it. He entered the dusty space and went straight for the single computer set up beside the long row of filing cabinets. Time to write reports for what had happened today. Send an email to his contact at ATF, Leo, about the guns.

Lord willing, the end of the day would go better than the beginning.

Kinsley awoke with a start, her mouth bone dry and eyes gritty. She rubbed them until her vision cleared.

Where was she? With Jasper. At the Tunnel Creek Police Station.

The fingers of one hand curled into fur. *Dash.* He lay on the rug along the front of the couch where she'd collapsed. Warmth unfurled in her chest. Keeping watch over her?

A door closed down the hall, and she pulled herself upright on the sagging leather couch. She must've slept for at least an hour, because the light outside had changed. Dimmed.

Where was Jasper?

The soft *smack* of footsteps neared, but the dog was at ease, his eyes trained on the door, head laying across his front paws.

Jasper appeared in the half-open doorway. "Hey, sleepyhead. How was your nap?"

"Long, apparently."

He entered the room, a stack of green files tucked under one arm. "It's been a little over an hour. Officer Anders is back on patrol, and I've got some paperwork to go through after we get your aunt's things."

He crossed the room, dropping to the cushion beside her. Her groggy nerves flickered at his rugged profile and closeness.

She blinked at him, then at the files. "What did you find?"

"For starters, I couldn't find your aunt's accident file."

"Maybe it was misplaced. Or misfiled. Or not filed yet." She curled her fingers together. It had only happened recently, after all.

"I wondered that, too. I'll ask around." He screwed his mouth up at one side. "I also checked for your parents' accident file."

She startled. "Why?"

"What if all this ties together, Kinsley?"

"I don't think so."

"Maybe I want to help you get rid of all that guilt." He reached out, catching a piece of her loose hair and rubbing it between his fingers. Warmth spiraled in her stomach. When he dropped the tendril, his surprised gaze shot to hers. "Your dad was driving that night, right?"

She sat there, immobilized. Finally, she nodded.

"Like it or not, the blame rests on him. If he wasn't—"

"It was about you. About us."

"What was?"

"The argument I had with my parents that night, in the car." Her heart sank like a stone as his earnest expression chilled. "It was about you."

"About me? Why?"

She hated to hurt him. "I'd been out with you that night, remember? We saw a movie at the drive-in. My dad had worked late, and when he got home at ten thirty, mom told him I was out with you. Then they picked me up from the movie. The accident happened on the way home. We had…" She gulped, hating that this would hurt him. "We argued about you before."

Hurt flickered over his face. "They didn't want you dating me."

"No, they didn't. But it wasn't personal against you. They didn't want me getting serious at such a young age. They wanted…" She licked her lips. "They wanted me to get out of Tunnel Creek, go to college." Which she had. And now she was on the cusp of achieving her next career objective: lead director of mammals. Discovering and studying a colony of bats in the Southeast would practically guarantee her the position.

Jasper was silent for several moments before continuing. "Before I forget, I did make a call to Atlanta, to your zoo again, asked to speak to Marta. She took personal leave. Did you know about that?"

*Leave?* "No, I don't remember her mentioning that." How could she afford to not work?

"Your supervisor gave me her direct cell. I'll try again. I already left one message."

"I don't know how she's able to afford to take a leave of absence. Unless it's paid leave."

"Could be. I'll stay on that." He stood, stretching side to side. "You ready to go to Anderson's?"

"Yes." Eagerness and dread twisted her insides as she rose.

He checked then pocketed a small black cell.

She cocked her head. "Did you get a different phone?"

"Yeah, this one's a loaner. Until I get my old one fixed."

Kinsley grabbed her bag and her water and followed him into the hallway. Her legs tingled and her heart pounded. What paperwork was in Aunt Rhonda's bag—and would they finally figure out why these men were after her?

# TWELVE

The humid air smothered them as they exited the station. The parking lot sat empty except for two squad cars and a massive blue truck at the far end.

She squinted at the driver. "Is that Noah?"

"Yeah. He's letting me borrow his truck. I'll drop him and Dash off at the cabin before we head to the funeral home."

Jasper wiped the sweat from his brow. Summer in South Carolina, even in the mountains, meant hot days and sticky nights. Dash trotted into the grass to the left of the building, sniffing the bushes and leaving behind doggy signs that he'd been there.

"It's about time," Noah called out through the open window before unlocking the doors.

"Want the front?" Jasper asked Kinsley.

"It's okay. I'll sit in the back with Dash."

Jasper loaded her and the dog inside, then climbed into the front and buckled his seat belt. His brother steered the lumbering vehicle out of the parking lot.

Noah dove right in. "That text you sent. You're serious about a hidden room in the Whisper Mountain Tunnel?"

"Dead serious." Jasper set his elbow on the console.

Soft country music played through the cab. "And we found guns in there. I just finished the report. Messaged my contact at ATF."

Noah let out a long, loud whistle. Dash whined in the back seat, pushing his cold nose into Jasper's neck.

"It's okay, boy." Jasper glanced at his brother. "Are you thinking what I'm thinking?"

"You and Mr. Tuttle. A gun-smuggling ring that didn't want their operation discovered."

"Exactly." Jasper gave a definitive nod. "Once I get my phone working again, I'll show you."

"You got pictures?"

"Yep, but my cell got damaged when we were shot at. I left that phone for the tech guys to work on tomorrow. I've got a dozen pictures or so. It was dark, but hopefully the auto flash will help show what was in those boxes."

"And you said someone followed you in there?"

Kinsley spoke up. "They did, but the person didn't seem to know about the hidden room." She addressed Jasper. "Do you think they did, Jasper?"

"Hard to say. But my guess is no, or they would've checked that space as well."

Traffic was light, so they made it through town quickly. In the distance, the retreating storm rumbled over the mountains, lightning flashes splintering the clouds. He'd always loved getting lost in the woods and living in the country, but with Kinsley's life in danger, killers on the loose and guns being smuggled in his town, things were way off-kilter. Now the forest he loved felt like it was closing in on them.

Noah released a hard breath. "Any ideas who's heading this operation?"

"I'm not sure. Someone who knows a lot about Tunnel Creek, because they found the perfect hiding spot."

His brother glanced into his rearview mirror at Kinsley. "How're you holding up?"

"I took a nap at the station, so at least I'm thinking straight now." She hesitated. "I'm glad your brother is here to help me. I've lost track of how many times he's saved me."

"He's good at that." Noah switched the radio off. "It's terrible, all this bad stuff that has happened now that you're back here."

"I'm not staying," she blurted out. "I mean, I'm here for my aunt's memorial, then I'll do some observation work and go back home." A weighty pause followed. "To Atlanta."

"Gotcha." Noah glanced at Jasper, then back at her. "Small-town life isn't for you, huh?"

"It's not..." Seconds ticked by as Kinsley seemed to struggle with answering Noah. "It's not really that. It's more for the career opportunities in Atlanta. Tunnel Creek doesn't provide those." Her voice shrank at the end.

"I get it." Noah shot a loaded sideways look at Jasper before addressing him. "So, how does all this gun stuff tie into Kinsley's situation?"

"Not sure yet, but I'm starting to wonder if her aunt found out about the illegal activity."

"How?" Kinsley asked.

"That's the million-dollar question. Once we get the file from the funeral home, I hope we'll figure that out."

"Did you pull Rhonda Miller's accident report at the station?" Noah asked.

"I tried. Couldn't find it."

"Still in processing, maybe." Noah drummed his fingers on the wheel. "I think you're onto something really risky here, Jas. Be careful. There's no telling how much money's wrapped up in those guns."

Noah steered up the driveway. From the ridge above, the cabin lights appeared like a lighthouse beacon. *Gabe.* Jasper couldn't wait to wrap his arms around his son tomorrow morning.

Noah parked and opened his door. "Think you need to call in the FBI?"

"I do. But first Kinsley and I are going to retrieve some of her aunt's items at Anderson's. I guess there were files in a purse or bag of some sort."

"Keep me posted. I'm here if you need me." Noah climbed out.

Jasper exited the cab, too. He sent Dash on his way inside and waved to his mom as Noah climbed the steps and turned around.

"Take care, brother," Noah called. "Watch your back." He draped an arm over their mom's shoulders as the pair watched them leave.

"Will do." He folded inside the truck and shifted into Reverse.

Kinsley had climbed into the front seat. "Your family is wonderful." Wistfulness was wrapped around her words. *Family.* Something she no longer had.

"They are pretty great."

"How's Brielle doing?"

He reached the end of the driveway, checked for oncoming traffic and headed back into town. "Brielle is busy." He made a face. "She owns the Antique Depot over on 64, just outside Tunnel Creek. I think she's in Asheville right now on a buying trip."

"Wow, good for her. We were partners in art class

junior year. She was always so talented with arts and crafts projects."

"Is that a nice way of saying she's good at making messes? Because that's what happens when she gets a hold of a piece of furniture."

"Ha. Maybe so. But messes for a profit are worthwhile."

"That's true. I just wish she'd stop over more. Gabe asks about her all the time."

"Brielle doesn't come to your place much?"

He shook his head. "Like I said, she's busy." His gaze remained on the road and on the rearview mirror. So far, no company. *Thank You, Lord.*

Ten minutes later they arrived at the imposing three-story house turned family business of Tunnel Creek's only funeral home. The structure stared at them with large rectangular windows and white eaves. A square white sign identified the building as "Anderson's Funeral Home," and a huge wraparound porch jutted out like a wooden brown beard.

Jasper drove past, pulling into the dry cleaner's parking lot next door instead.

"What're you doing?" She twisted in her seat. "We just passed it."

"I'm parking at a different place. I want to keep this visit on the down low for now."

Jasper parked the truck and climbed out. His weapon felt like a rock lodged in his holster, and his pulse beat a heavy rhythm in his eardrums. This was it. Finally. Something concrete that would help them solve this case. Did any of the men after Kinsley know of the file's location?

"Amy Anderson said the items might be in the lockbox out back."

"Let's check inside first. Make sure they know you retrieved them."

She gave a jerky nod, then fell into step with him. His arm brushed hers as they climbed the front steps and crossed the porch. A pair of rocking chairs creaked slowly in the breeze. A little hanging sign said "Open, Come On In." Jasper crossed in front of Kinsley and opened the door for her, then followed close behind. The foyer was two stories high and the size of the cabin's front room.

"Wow, I feel like I just stepped into the 1970s," Kinsley whispered.

"They haven't changed much around here." He motioned her down the hallway to the office area. He'd been here enough times, on duty and for townspeople, that he knew his way around. His chest caved in. Not to mention Willard Tuttle's service.

The large room at the center of the house served as an office during business hours and a refreshment area during memorials. Jasper entered, searching for Amy Anderson or her younger brother, Timothy, who worked the phone and reception area for their parents.

Jasper noticed two things immediately. First, the tan couch, three chairs and large round table were empty; and second, no one was standing behind the reception desk. Strange.

"What—oh my." Kinsley pressed her fingers to her mouth.

The floor around the desk and counter was covered in papers and file folders, pens and office supplies. Manila folders and writing utensils littered the carpet, and upended boxes lay along the wall beside the counter. A chair had been thrown sideways.

The hair on the back of Jasper's neck stood on end. "Someone's been here."

"What do we do?"

He measured the space. Three closed doors sat on the two far walls. One was a bathroom; the second door led to the back processing area; and the third was a bedroom-sized storage closet, where Frank Anderson and his family kept extra chairs for viewings and services.

"Stay close." He settled a hand on his weapon and pointed to the front desk with the other. She nodded, moving forward with him like they were in a three-legged race. He strained to hear any unusual noises. *There.* Muted, labored breathing. Where—

A thump sounded on the other side of the counter. From underneath. Jasper rushed toward it, weapon drawn and safety off. Kinsley gasped as a young man rolled out from under the desk, his mouth taped shut and his hands bound together.

Timothy Anderson. Jasper waved at Timothy, then pivoted, scrutinizing the room.

"Kins, get the tape off his mouth."

She edged forward and sank to her knees. "I'm sorry..." She grimaced, then pulled.

Timothy moaned but shook his head as Kinsley pulled the tape off. Blood crusted under his nose, and a purple bruise was encircling his left eye.

She worked at the tape around his wrists next.

"Officer Holt, I'm so glad to see you."

Jasper slashed his hand across his mouth to tell him to be quiet, then gestured to ask which door the perp had hidden behind.

Timothy bared his teeth in a grimace, raising both shoulders and shaking his head. He didn't know. Jasper edged around him and crept toward the closet and storage room. It made the most sense. The man could've climbed in and out of the window, which was on the side of the house, and the room offered multiple places to hide.

A crashing noise erupted behind Jasper, and Kinsley screamed as a black-clad figure burst out of the bathroom door. Straight for her. The man had one arm around her neck, yielding a dagger knife in the other in two seconds flat. The shiny weapon sent lightning through Jasper's veins.

Jasper lunged forward, sweeping a leg out and unbalancing the perp. The man stumbled backward, sending the knife through the air. It clattered to the floor in front of the countertop. Timothy ducked and snatched it away as Jasper clutched Kinsley's arm, disengaging her from the perp's loose hold.

"Hang on!" He swung her like he did Gabe, and she sailed in a semicircle from the momentum, landing on the couch with a grunt. She might have a bruise, but at least she was away from that knife and the assailant. Jasper had his weapon trained on the man the next second.

"Hands up," he shouted. "I said, put them up! Keep them there. You have the right to remain silent. Anything you say or do—"

The man spit at him.

Jasper subdued him, holding the perp's arms behind his back to finish telling him his rights. If only he'd brought his cuffs.

"I'm not saying anything to you." Then the man sneered at Kinsley, who huddled on the couch. "Your time's up, lady."

"Timothy, call 911. Tell the dispatcher I'm here and what happened." The younger man tugged out his phone and did as Jasper asked. Jasper barely held his temper in check as the perp continued spewing threats at Kinsley. He met her eyes across the funeral home's office. Her chest rose and fell, and their gazes clung. She wore a wary, wounded expression. Like one of the animals she helped save.

A powerful emotion clocked him at the thought of that knife near her throat.

*Adrenaline. Relief.* That was it. He just needed to get her safely back to his mom's.

Ten minutes later Jasper watched Officer Anders pull away, the attacker cuffed in the back seat, still spewing ugly threats. Jasper told Chris he'd return to the station shortly.

Jasper took the funeral home–porch steps in one bound and stepped back inside the front entryway. Timothy stood with Kinsley and Frank Anderson beside a paramedic. Frank had arrived minutes ago, and the EMTs had come right after Officer Anders.

"How're you holding up, Timothy?" Jasper asked the twenty-one-year-old.

"I think I'm finally ready to take those self-defense classes you keep telling me about." He shoved a hand through his shaggy hair. "What was that guy after?"

Jasper shook his head. "I can't disclose that at this time. The investigation is still ongoing."

Frank Anderson finished speaking with someone on his cell phone, then joined the conversation. "Officer Holt, Amy placed the items for Kinsley Miller in the lockbox. We weren't sure when she would be coming to get the personal items. I hope it's not a problem."

"Not a problem at all. I came inside to make sure you all were aware Ms. Miller was retrieving them."

Frank ran his fingers over his bald head. "I'll get

those items for you. Be right back." He stepped through the back hallway.

Jasper set a hand on Kinsley's upper arm. "You all right? I hope I wasn't too rough when I tossed you onto the couch."

"I'm okay." She touched the bandage on her forehead. "You could've thrown me headfirst, and I wouldn't have minded. I just wanted to get away from that guy."

The thud of footsteps carried up the stairs and clomped down the hall. Jasper and Kinsley stared as a breathless Frank returned.

"I can't believe my eyes. This has never happened. Why would—"

He stopped, chest heaving, trying to catch his breath.

"What is it?" Jasper's hand fell to his weapon.

"Well, it appears someone used a heavy-duty tool to break into the lockbox. I'm sorry, Ms. Miller, but the items are missing."

Kinsley stood at the guest bedroom window in the cabin, the chorus of crickets and the hooting owl nearby failing to calm her jumpy pulse. Night had fallen, and she longed to feel as peaceful as the nocturnal creatures sounded. Instead, her thoughts skipped back to the fight at the funeral home and Frank Anderson's shocked expression.

*...the items are missing...*

A breeze whistled past, forcing a branch against the glass. The scraping frazzled her nerves and kept sleep at bay. She set her shoulder to the wall and peered out the window. The lack of light pollution in Tunnel Creek created an exquisite canvas showcasing God's creation. A verse from Vacation Bible School lit up her mind in the darkness:

*And God made two great lights; the greater light to rule the day, and the lesser light to rule the night: he made the stars also. And God set them in the firmament of the heaven to give light upon the earth.*

A tiny movement caught her eye in the inky night sky.

Kinsley straightened. A bat! Then another. She followed their jagged motions as they jettisoned through the air like tiny airplanes, darting and diving for insects.

Were these the bats from the grist mill? It wasn't too far from here. Kinsley craned her neck, blinking to make out their compact forms and acrobatic movements as they devoured their dinner. From the cabin's second floor, she glimpsed the area of the mountain where the tunnel was, though in summer it was nearly impossible to see through the foliage.

Surely the God who had made the sun and the moon would help guide her and Jasper to the end of this case. Show them the answers they desperately needed. *Please, Lord. We need Your help.*

Something flickered in the distance.

Was that a light? Could it be at the ranger station?

Kinsley squinted hard, dropping her chin to her chest to focus. She must be seeing things.

She returned her focus to the bats. But they were gone now, likely moved on to a different area to feed or resting in the trees.

There it was again! The light. Except this time, the tiny yellow spot remained on, stationary. She held the curtain back and pressed her forehead to the glass. Several seconds passed as she stared at the unnatural yellow mark in the forest. Then it shut off.

Who was up at the Whisper Mountain Tunnel now? Jasper had mentioned getting in touch with other law enforcement branches to handle this. Could it be ATF agents out there for the guns?

A knock sounded at her bedroom door, and she dropped the curtain and turned.

"Kinsley, are you awake?"

*Jasper.* She released a strained breath and padded across the room to let him in.

He filled the doorway, and her mind went to what she'd just seen.

She spoke at the same time he did. "I just saw a light out at the tunnel."

"My phone is MIA."

Kinsley dropped her chin. "What?"

"Did you say you saw something out there? You're sure?"

"You go first." She touched her redressed bandage gingerly. "Your phone's missing?"

He strode across the room. "Yes. It's gone. I left it on Maddox's desk. He's our tech guy. I looked all over. Officer Anders took the man we arrested to book him at the jail. I stayed, checked everywhere." Jasper fisted his hands. "I'm wondering if this is an inside job."

She bent over to straighten the rug. "You mean another officer?"

"I don't know. Maybe." He rammed a hand through his hair. "Or maybe my mind is playing tricks on me, and I left the phone somewhere else."

"No, I remember you told me you left it there."

He turned abruptly to pace the room again. "It'll turn up. So, the light at the tunnel, you're sure it wasn't a car driving through the forest?"

"I don't think so. This light was stationary and seemed unnatural. Man-made, I mean. Could it be the other officer you contacted, the ATF?"

"I don't think so. Leo said he'd let me know when they were heading in to retrieve them." He strode over to the window, staring into the dark.

"Did you learn anything about the man who came after us at Anderson's?"

He turned to face her. "He's from Greenville. Has prior arrests. Mostly minor stuff. Petty theft and bounced checks. Stole a car a few years back."

A buzz sounded from Jasper's pocket. He tugged out the loaner cell and clicked on the screen. "Holt here."

Several seconds of *uh-huhs* and weighty pauses followed. One murmured "Great news" piqued her curiosity, so she inched closer. Kinsley held on to every nuance, taking in Jasper's broad back and animated gestures.

He tapped End, then spun around, excitement bannered on his face. "We've got a winner."

"A winner? Finally, some good news!" She grabbed his hands, squeezing his palms impatiently. They both stared down at the two points of connection, and her stomach jumped. She released her hold on him. "Sorry."

"Don't be. That was Officer Anders. He just pulled over a speeder on the other side of town. Guess what Chris found in the trunk?"

Kinsley sucked in a breath. "The items from the funeral home?"

"Exactly. He found a cache of files and a large tan purse belonging to a Rhonda Miller."

"Thank You, Lord," she pressed a palm to her heart. "What happens next?"

"I'll head back to the station to sort all this out. Technically, it's closed for the night, but I'm not wasting any more time before I get a look at the file. Plus, I still need to comb through your dad's paperwork. *You* better get some sleep."

"My nap earlier did me in." She grimaced. Not the best expression to use, given the situation. "I mean, I can't sleep. Please, let me come in with you."

"I don't think that's wise. I'm going to swing by the tunnel and make sure nothing's going on up there first."

"Are you taking Dash?"

He shook his head. "Not tonight. He's been favoring his front leg a bit and needs rest."

"Let *me* come. Please, Jasper."

Seconds passed, his legs shifting as he inched toward the door. She noticed the moment his shoulders drooped in defeat. "You'll follow my directions? Do exactly what I tell you to do, when I tell you to do it?"

She tiptoed over to grasp his hands again. His bold warmth flowed into her, shocking and comforting all at once. "I will. I promise."

His thumbs stroked over hers, once. Twice. Enough that a charged energy flooded her veins. "Jasper?"

One of his hands freed from her hold and traced the bandage on the side of her forehead. "Is this healing okay?"

"I think so. The wound itches a lot. Hopefully, it won't leave a scar."

"It won't matter."

She tilted her head. "What do you mean?"

"You're beautiful with or without a scar."

She tucked in her chin to hide the smile lifting her mouth. His matter-of-fact comment settled deep inside, and she worried she'd never forget how his voice rumbled when he said it.

"I don't like bossing you around, Kinsley. I'm just trying to keep you alive."

"I know." She lifted her gaze, meeting his dark, solemn eyes. "I can't think of a better person to be on my side."

He gave her a single nod and withdrew his fingers. "Meet me downstairs in five minutes."

Then he disappeared into the hallway, leaving her alone with the fact that Jasper might be a danger to her after all.

*No*, she told herself. She was *this* close—a bat's wingbeat close—to achieving lead director at her zoo. How could she give all that up? And worse—*she* was a danger to Jasper and his sweet young son. She pictured Gabriel, his innocent enthusiasm as she'd taught him about the lizard. Felt his little hand in hers as they said goodbye to Lizzy the blue-tailed skink.

What if the men got to him?

She shook her head as her stomach twisted. *No*. The sooner she was gone from their lives, the better.

# THIRTEEN

Jasper steered Noah's truck onto the shoulder, easing it down the embankment so it was hidden from the road. Kinsley sat like a statue beside him. In this spot, the vehicle was hidden from sight, and it gave them easy access—via a strenuous ten-minute hike—to a perch overlooking the entrance to Whisper Mountain Tunnel.

They'd likely not find anything out here tonight, but it was worth checking. Jasper had texted Noah his location then messaged Officer Hammond for backup.

*Please, Lord. Guide my steps. Keep us safe.*

Hope had cleared away the cobwebs in his mind. They had secured the items from Rhonda Miller, which Officer Anders was delivering to the office any moment. Jasper could hardly wait to take a look at it. Solve the mystery, catch these criminals. Then Kinsley was free to return home to her big city and forget about Tunnel Creek—and him—once and for all.

It was for the best.

He squared his shoulders, pulled his mind back to the case. In all there were at least three perps who'd been sent after Kinsley. Her hotel kidnapper was still at large, as far as he knew. His vision dimmed. What kind of operation utilized so many men?

Still, this had to mean a breakthrough on the case. Even with the two arrested men pleading the Fifth and hiring lawyers, the district attorney would get to the bottom of this.

Jasper's mind snagged on that word…*attorney*.

"Your dad was an attorney."

"Right." She clicked her seat belt loose. "He had his own small criminal defense firm."

What if…?

Was he grasping at straws? "Hear me out. What if your dad uncovered something years ago about whoever is involved with these guns and—"

"My mom and dad's accident wasn't an accident," she finished in a whisper, yet the words still filled the truck's cab. "But that was years ago."

He gnawed the inside of his cheek. "Maybe there's something else tying them together."

"All of this has brought back a strange memory. One of the officers who interviewed me the morning after their accident made this off-hand comment to another officer. I overheard it. It was along the lines of 'The second car must've swung out of its way to hit the Millers' car.' Something like that? I don't know, Jasper. It seemed odd for them to say that, but I was half–out of it because of pain medication and grief. I'm still not sure I heard them right."

"You probably did. I'll add that to your testimony when we're back at the station."

They exited the truck, and he circled the back of the vehicle to meet her by the woods. Night insects set up a racket, competing with the constant whistle of the breeze. Jasper strained to hear any other noises.

He patted down his pockets and waistband, which

contained his weapon and a flashlight. "Did you grab the other flashlight in the door?"

"Got it." She swung the silver device in the air.

"One more thing…" He pointed at the front driver-side door. "If you ever need it, there's a small pistol in the glove compartment. The key to start the truck and open the glove compartment is taped to the underside of the seat you were sitting in."

She gaped at him like the thought of holding a gun scared the daylights out of her. "Alright."

"What, you can pick up lizards and spiders just fine, but a handgun will do you in?"

"Well, yes. Animals don't shoot bullets. And when have I ever picked up a spider?"

"Homeroom, eleventh grade? The teacher was about to kill it, and you wanted to save it." He gave a soft whistle. "You had me at 'I'll get it.' I knew right then and there you were the girl for me."

"Stop it." Kinsley giggled, and his breath hitched in his chest. It was like hearing sunshine sing.

"Hey, didn't your dad make you take that gun-safety class right before we graduated, anyway?"

Kinsley nodded slowly, her grin slipping away. Her eyes flickered over his face, surprise in their depths. Did she have the same thought he just did?

*Why had her dad insisted on that class—right before the accident?*

He broke off staring at her and instead looked around, getting his bearings. He and Dash had hiked the area that circled Whisper Mountain Tunnel at least two dozen times but never at night. Still, the trail would be their best chance at seeing any activity near the tunnel while remaining under cover.

He motioned toward the entry into the woods. "That's the spot. Stay close."

They set off, Jasper in the lead, Kinsley right behind him. She was as sure-footed in the woods as he. Probably more so. Moonlight shone through the trees, holding back the darkness.

They followed the narrow, twisting trail for several minutes. She was doing everything he'd told her to— silent steps, quiet breathing, staying close. As they ascended a rise with thinned-out foliage, he slowed and turned, motioning for her to crouch.

He edged in until they were only inches apart. "We're almost to the tunnel side of the mountain. We have to slow down and watch our noise. So far, you're the best partner I've had." He winked at her, and her eyes crinkled in the corners with a smile.

"Not as good at Dash."

"I don't know. He drools and snores." Her hand caught his arm, giving a gentle squeeze. "What is it?" He was buzzing with adrenaline, and holding still for this long made his limbs shake.

"Do any other officers know we're here?"

"Officer Hammond should be on his way."

"Good." She paused. "Thank you for letting me come along. And for keeping me safe."

The urge to say *anytime* came swiftly, then left just as fast. Having her with him felt like an emotional contradiction. He enjoyed her company but hated that she was in danger.

What would it be like if they were together *without* this trouble, without any fear of who was trying to kill her hanging over their heads?

Jasper slammed the door on that thought. She couldn't be clearer that she wanted out of Tunnel Creek as soon as the memorial service and her animal-saving work were over. Besides, his job now—along with law enforcement—was to protect Gabe. Physically and emotionally. And his son was already enamored with the sweet young woman who loved critters, too.

Kinsley Miller didn't belong here. Better to get this case solved and return to normal life.

They pushed deeper into the woods, sidestepping trees and rocks and blackberry thickets. A startled possum waddled away, and the chirp of crickets quieted near their feet.

"So, how is it, working in a zoo?"

Kinsley sighed. Not the response he expected.

"I thought you loved your job."

"I do," she answered immediately. "My work brings me so much satisfaction. The animals do. Figuring out ways to keep wildlife safe. Improving their habitats. Studying their behavior. Figuring out how and why animals return to the areas they were birthed in. Playing a role in increasing threatened animals' numbers. All of it." She paused. "But…"

"But…"

"I spend all day caring for animals. Mostly I'm…"

"Happy."

"Yes. And lonely."

Surprise sifted through him like sunlight through a canopy of trees. What she admitted held a mirror up to his own life. Was he lonely, too? He had his family. Gabe, Mom, Noah. Brielle, when she came over. His work fulfilled him. Helping people, rescuing pet birds, catching criminals.

But yeah… Sometimes it felt like something was missing.

He focused back on the ground beneath his feet.

Reality. The elevation angled upward on the trail, and their breathing came heavier. They had to slow down to keep the volume low. His boot slipped on the damp ground. Another line of storms was expected in the area the next day.

"Hold up." He hitched his stride to a halt. "There's the Triplets."

"What?"

"Those big rocks." He pointed to the ten-foot wall of three large boulders crammed together. "Let's rest here for a minute. It's a good hiding spot, too."

"If we see someone down there, near the tunnel, can you record them?"

He shook his head. "It'd be inadmissible in court. Can't record without consent from at least one person involved in the conversation. But I can try to take pictures. And we'll both serve as eyewitnesses."

He peered down the hill, through the trees. Shadows shifted, stretching across the tunnel. He hated to get too close, but they needed to move forward to be in eye and earshot.

Jasper motioned her past the Triplets, and they slipped through the thickets behind the large rocks to catch their breath. A June bug bumped his forehead, and he flicked it away. They continued around Whisper Mountain, moving with slow-motion steps until they were within a couple hundred yards of the tunnel's mouth. Jasper stopped, held up a hand.

"I don't think it's possible, but in case they can hear us walking overhead—with them underneath, inside the tunnel, I mean—let's go further up."

She tailed closely as he clambered higher, scaling the damp rocky ground. Shoving back ferns and brambles and broken branches brought down by yesterday's storm. His chest heaved, and he struggled to keep his breathing quiet as they found a spot no longer overtop or near the entrance to the tunnel. He circled behind a thicket surrounding a large rock, and he waved at her to follow. Then Jasper crouched, his knees sinking into the dirt. Kinsley sank beside him.

They both wiped sweat from their brows.

He pointed. "There's a clearing up ahead. About ten feet away. It looks directly over the entrance. You stay here, beneath the thicket. Let me see if there's any activity down below."

"Can't we both go check?"

He shook his head. "Stay put. You're hidden here. I'll be right back."

"No. I'm coming, too."

He scrubbed a hand down his face. "Talk about irony. You wanted nothing to do with me ten years ago. You left Tunnel Creek—and me—and never looked back. Now I can't get you unglued from my side, even when we're in a risky situation."

"Jasper, I didn't end things with you because of *you*. I ended them because of me."

A whirlwind of anger swept through his chest. "If that isn't a canned answer, I don't know what is."

"It's not canned. It's the truth. I did care about you." She looked away. "But Tunnel Creek held so many memories, and with my parents' deaths and feeling like I was responsible, it felt like a pit of sinking sand—guilt I couldn't escape fast enough. Then when I did, I didn't want to come back."

"I get it, Kinsley. That's all in the past. Let's just leave it at that."

She nodded, and he turned away. He shouldn't have

brought her. He was better off working alone. "You ready, then?"

"Yes."

"Keep low, watch where you step. If something gives us away, run straight around the mountain, then down it. Then east. Get to the truck and contact Noah."

"Okay." Her voice wavered.

"You don't have to do this."

"I know." She looked down, then back at him. "I'm tired of being scared."

He cupped her cheek briefly, her skin warm and soft beneath his palm. They stared at each other for several intense seconds, then he dropped his hand. *Focus, Holt.* He pivoted and crept forward. The edge of the clearing in front of the tunnel came into view, cloaked by night. Five more feet.

He reached the cluster of bushes, flinching when one bramble pierced his shirt and jabbed his skin. Thick mud slurped beneath his boots. Kinsley followed silently. A frog croaked nearby, then stopped when they sank to their heels beside the shrubs.

He tugged his binoculars from around his neck and uncapped them. They weren't thermal, so it was difficult to make out much of the surroundings forty yards down, across the face of the tunnel. He lowered the binoculars and used his shirt to wipe the smudged lenses. Gabe must've gotten his sticky fingers on them recently.

"Maybe we missed them," Kinsley whispered. "Or maybe my imagination got the best of me at the cabin."

"We're about to find out."

He placed the binoculars to his face again. A movement through the lens snagged his attention. He turned to his left about ten degrees, near the tunnel entrance. Someone was walking out, holding a large duffel bag.

"You were right. There's activity."

She tensed against him. "Do you want me to take pictures with your cell?"

"You can try, but without flash, the images will be grainy." He slid the loaner device to her, typing in his code. She set it to her face, and he returned his gaze downward. Where was the man carrying the bag heading? There. A glint of metal and then wheels. A dolly. Make that two. And a larger vehicle. A four-wheeler, maybe? It could make that trail no problem.

Kinsley wobbled, and he shot out his free arm to steady her.

"I'm getting a bunch of pictures, but I don't know if we'll be able to see anything."

A twig snapped behind them, and Jasper jumped up and whipped around. Too late. Two men converged on them, their faces hidden by shadows. Kinsley gasped, ducking away as one of the men grabbed for her. Jasper launched into him, and their collision knocked into the second man, bringing all three of them down. Jasper released his arms from the man's middle and twisted so he had a choke hold on him. His heart pounded in his ears.

"Run!" he shouted at her. "Go!"

The second man struggled to stand. Kinsley leaped over them and dashed through the woods.

"Run!" he yelled again, tightening his arm around the man's windpipe.

The man in the choke hold no longer struggled, but the second man hovered over Jasper, breathing hard and growling as he circled him, bulky arms spread like wings.

Jasper disentangled himself from the subdued attacker and rose to meet the second man.

"What'd you do to Mike"

"Who's Mike? That guy?" Jasper pointed to his unconscious choke hold victim, distracting him for a split second, then darted in to lay a jab on the man's throat. The attacker jerked sideways, and the hit only took halfway. Still, he coughed and moaned, struggling backward. No time to waste. Jasper was on him, shoving them both toward the rocks they'd crouched beside.

He had the man on his back in two seconds, then grabbed an arm and yanked it toward him. Arm bars always came in handy. The perp cried out in pain as the hold hyperextended. He almost had him. A crunch behind them snatched Jasper's focus. Another perp?

"Jasper Holt, you're a hard man to hold down."

Jasper jumped to his feet at the sound of that voice. Everything spun. Who…?

Officer Dean Hammond stood four feet away, his nightstick at the ready. He was in plain clothes and didn't advance on Jasper. Instead, Dean stood there, taking in the two incapacitated men on the ground with a strange, gloating expression.

"Hammond. You want to help me get them cuffed?"

"I'm afraid that's not gonna happen today."

A black hole opened up in Jasper's gut. "Dean. Tell me you're not part of this."

"See, the thing is, I can't do that."

Jasper fought the urge to clench his eyes shut and throw his head back. How long had he known Dean? Joked with him at work? Played ball with him on their days off?

"Sure, Mr. Officer of the Year. Act like you're surprised. But you have no clue what my life is like. How else am I going to pay off my fiancée's debts? She's gonna lose her house, and they repossessed her car." He spit on the ground. "If her stupid ex-husband hadn't left town and quit paying child support, I wouldn't have gotten involved when he asked."

"When *who* asked?"

Hammond blew past the question. "Man, why do you have to be so thick?"

Jasper pressed his palms to his thighs to keep from using them on Hammond. He needed to buy time and get answers. "Must've been kind of rough, killing Kinsley's aunt Rhonda."

Dean startled, then glared at him. "Shut up. You have no idea what happened that night."

Jasper pulled his lips into his teeth. "Who's giving you orders?"

"Like I'm going tell you. You weren't even supposed to be part of this." Dean stepped forward, shoving his finger at Jasper. "But you had to get in the middle of everything to save *her*."

"One of us had to do our job. The one where we swore an oath to protect the citizens of this town."

"You know what? I'm done talking." Dean rushed in, swinging. Jasper ducked, but it was too late. Another shadow blurred in his peripheral vision. A fourth man? A painful *thud* rang through his ears and reverberated from his skull down through his body. Darkness swallowed him whole.

Branches clawed her face and rocks scraped her legs as Kinsley hurtled through the woods. Fear nipped at her heels, too. And guilt. What had happened to Jasper? Was he okay? She could still hear the echo of his voice shouting at her to run, the thud of a fist hitting his flesh.

*Please, God, protect Jasper. Watch over him.* The ragged prayer fell to the earth as she barreled onward. Was she going in the right direction? She ran through the directions Jasper gave her earlier, but none of her surroundings made any sense. The terrain descended, but it didn't look familiar. They hadn't come this way.

She shoved through a last line of thickets and came upon a clearing dotted with a few trees. Bending in half, she gulped breaths of muggy air. Her heart thundered in her chest. After checking multiple times to see if anyone was coming behind her, she jogged forward. Wildflowers waved softly under a canopy of stars.

The beautiful scene was obliterated by the harsh reality that Jasper was in grave danger.

The faint sound of a man's voice carried off the mountain. Stalking her. It wasn't Jasper. A sob erupted in her chest. What if he was—

*No.* She stopped the thought, stumbling forward.

Where was the road? They hadn't passed through a field of flowers on their way up and around Whisper Mountain.

An image of Gabe's sweet face filled her mind. *Jasper.* What if they killed him? Tears stung her eyes, trickled down her cheeks. The thought of losing him was a physical blow that took her breath away.

A shout reverberated across the clearing. Had one of them seen her?

Kinsley jumped over a rotted tree trunk, but her shoe caught on the top and she flew facedown, landing hard in the dirt. Grit and leaves stuck to her face and hands, and prickly vines poked her neck.

The stump was huge, at least a couple feet high at the peak. Beside it, the root system had rotted away, leaving a hollow space encased by ferns, stones and dead branches.

Her muscles stiffened as desperation grappled with reality. She had to hide.

Kinsley eyed the space beneath the stump. Did an animal already live there? A possum or raccoon? She didn't mind any of them but would rather not climb into their homes.

"No choice," she muttered, rolling sideways toward the hidden nook below the decrepit stump. Bits of soggy wood and moss clung to her neck, and a centipede slithered over her calf. She shivered at the sensation, then touched it to hurry it along. She carefully scooped out more space so her body was inside, covered in ferns, decaying wood and who-knows-what-else.

The voice closed in.

"I am looking. I know we gotta bring her back."

A man approached her hiding spot, his uneven, heavy steps betraying his size and physical abilities. No animal would make such a ruckus. Could she outrun him? Doubt wound around her nerves.

Her lungs constricted as the ground nearby vibrated with his footsteps. Her arms were partially crossed over her chest, hands curled to her neck. Sweat beaded her temples. Every few seconds, he slowed down, probably looking around.

*Please, God, cover any tracks I left behind.*

He tripped, thudding to the ground. An oath filled the quiet night as he struggled upright.

The earth above her shook, releasing dirt and bits of wood into her hair. The man was standing right overtop the stump. A scream tickled her throat, and her heart thrashed against her ribs.

What if he was heavy enough to push through the soggy, rotting wood? She'd be a goner for sure then since she was already buried. She trembled in the hole and found that her eyes had adjusted to the dark shelf-in-the-ground hiding place.

A rustle nearby sent liquid fire through her veins. She'd always been able to sense an animal's presence, and Kinsley knew without a doubt she was no longer alone in the hollow space. Something small but very much alive rested a foot or so from her body.

She held perfectly still. She'd probably entered a nocturnal animal's den, and now it had returned. Normally, this wouldn't bother her in the least—but normally, she wouldn't lay *inside* the den. She'd be outside, observing behavior and marking animal tracks, noting evidence of prey and proximity to other animals. The time of day it fed and slept and hunted.

Tonight, she was the one being hunted.

"I don't see her. She must've kept running."

Another voice answered, "He won't be happy if we come back empty-handed. He said to bring them both in."

She pressed a fist to her mouth. *Both?* So they already had Jasper?

The man near her hiding spot made another gross coughing sound before answering. "He's gonna have to deal with it. I don't see her."

Whatever was in the den with her stirred, rustling deeper inside, gently pushing down leaves and sticks. Slowly. Softly, with a definite sound pattern.

Goose bumps prickled her neck. If she wasn't mistaken, she was now lying in a snake's den, with a hired killer only a few yards away.

# FOURTEEN

Kinsley curled her legs slowly toward her stomach and kept her hands in front of her throat. If it was a venomous snake, she stood the best chance with a bite to her backside instead of near her vital organs, which was where the reptile currently lay.

Was the man nearby? She couldn't hear his voice, and he must've stopped moving. Kinsley eyed the opening to the wide, flat den. Ferns, dead sticks and twigs coated the ground like nature's carpet. She'd make a racket if she lunged out.

But staying inside wasn't ideal, especially if the snake was a copperhead. Her toes curled in her shoes. While their venom was much more deadly to rats and mice, she didn't care to test the theory at the moment.

The man's footsteps grew louder. Inside the den, leaves rustled, and a sharp hiss carried from the vicinity of her feet. Her lungs squeezed tight until her air was cut off. Could the snake's heat sensors locate her easily, or had the leaves and twigs covered enough of her body?

The man's footsteps carried in a tight circle around the tree stump. Each pound sent the snake into a shivering coil, closer and closer to her.

Kinsley bit the inside of her cheek as the snake slid

over her legs, the speed of its slithering increasing as the footsteps neared. Once it climbed over her body, the reptile coiled near the entrance, its head visible in the faint light trickling through the opening.

A copperhead. Her eyes widened as she drew in careful, steady breaths. It felt like her heart was part of a fireworks display in her chest. Right now, though, she had no choice but to stay still in the den.

During a college internship, when she'd had to deal with snakes—a grumpy python, in particular—she'd found that naming the animal made it less intimidating.

This fellow would be called Sam. *Sam the snake.*

The chime of a cell ringing broke the dismal line of thoughts. The man's voice boomed from right above Kinsley's hiding spot. With each syllable, the snake pulsed, its tail vibrating.

"Yeah, I'm still looking. No sign of her. I know, I'm hungry, too. Where are we meeting next, anyway?"

A pause.

"Why the Miller house?" He rumbled his dislike of that news. "There's no food. Yeah, whatever."

Her next breath jammed up in her windpipe. They were meeting at her old house? Where was the other officer Jasper had called in for backup?

The man stopped talking, shuffling around to the front of the den. Kinsley's stomach swooped around like a dragonfly caught inside a car. If he squatted down, he would see her.

"She's not here. Check the road into the tunnel." He rested a heavy leg on a decayed root outside the den, and the snake launched from its coiled position with a staccato hiss.

"Right, right. I'm heading back. I can't— Whoa!" he screamed, and the booming thud of a body hitting the ground shook the earth, raining down dirt and bits of wood into her face. The snake disappeared outside the den, and the man continued screeching and grunting as he stumbled away from the tree trunk.

Kinsley sucked in tiny gulps of oxygen as her lungs opened back up. Waiting a few minutes would be wiser, but she didn't want to risk being blocked in the snake's den again.

She peered around, but there was no sign of the irritable reptile. Crawling out, she kept low to the ground, then stood slowly, scanning the forest for the injured man. His form was only a stumbling shadow in the distance. They had Jasper. Was he hurt? Would they keep him alive?

Her tense muscles loosened, threatening to send her to the ground again. *No.* She would not believe he was dead. She refused to contemplate the dull ache that positioned itself in her heart at the thought of him being harmed. *Dead.* How could she ever forgive herself then?

She turned in a circle. Her instincts told her to head northwest to find Noah's truck. Among humans and concrete and buildings, her internal compass didn't work well. But here in Sumter National Forest, where she'd traipsed with her dad for hours and spent much of her childhood, she felt completely at home. And she was tired of denying it.

"Bye, Sam—wherever you are." Kinsley took off for the far side of the meadow.

Pain pulsated in Jasper's temples. He jerked awake, squinting against the constant throb. His head felt like it weighed a hundred pounds. Everything was dark. He wasn't outside anymore. But this wasn't the tunnel's hidden chamber, either. No, he was sitting in a formal seat—a dining room chair? His hands were bound together tightly behind him, ankles tied to the legs.

Wherever he tried to go, the chair would come along.

He blinked into the dim surroundings. Under his feet lay an expensive throw rug on a hardwood floor. A large dining room table filled the space across from where he sat, and what appeared to be an entryway connected the two rooms. The staircase to the second floor disappeared into a dark stairwell.

Jasper closed his eyes as the dots connected in his fuzzy brain.

He was in Kinsley's old house. His gut squeezed. Did they have her, too?

"He's waking up, boss."

Someone laughed, the sound hollow and cold. Jasper swiveled his head toward the stairs, where a man sprawled on the fourth stair up, an expensive weapon resting on his lap. He wore a ballcap over straggly brown hair. Muscles bulged beneath his clothes, and pricey sneakers squeaked against the wood floor when the gunman jumped down and made eye contact.

"Boss! He's awake."

It must've been one of the men Jasper had tussled with on Whisper Mountain, because a purple shiner gleamed from one eye and the skin on his neck was darkening to a bruise.

Footsteps sounded from the kitchen area, and a shadow appeared. When the person's face came into view, Jasper's jaw dropped.

Mayor David Barnhill strode into the entryway, hands clasped and face lit up like they were at a Christmas toy drive.

"Mayor Barnhill?" Bitterness soured on Jasper's tongue. "I'm disappointed to see you here." After all

these years, serving Tunnel Creek. Building a new play-
ground and a park in the center of town. Raising money
to expand the homeless shelter. Breaking ground on the
new hospice facility. Putting in a community pool and
offering a bus during the summer to reach low-income
kids who lived too far to walk.

Tunnel Creek's hometown hero was just the opposite. *The guns...?*

"I see you're drawing conclusions you have no right
to draw." Barnhill approached, his smile cooling into
a condescending smirk.

"I'd say I have every right to think the worst of you.
Where is she?"

"She'll turn up soon. Patience, my friend." Barnhill
pulled out another dining room chair and placed it in
front of Jasper's. He sat, his expensive suit wrinkled
and his shrewd eyes pinned to Jasper's face.

So they didn't have her yet. Clever Kinsley got away.
*Thank You, God.* "You're not my friend." How could
he have worked side by side with this man at charity
events? Waved to him at church? "I looked up to you.
Respected you."

"As you should."

How had Jasper never noticed the crookedness of
Barnhill's smile? "I have pictures of the weapons on
my phone."

"How convenient that Officer Hammond retrieved
that for me. Consider it destroyed."

Did Kinsley still have his loaner phone, with the pictures from the tunnel she just took? *If* they even turned
out clear enough to see. Jasper wasn't mentioning it.
"You don't care about anything or anyone except money
and power," Jasper muttered. "You're just a criminal
hiding in expensive clothes."

"Watch yourself, or your eccentric mother and that little boy of yours might step into my crosshairs, too."

Red tinted Jasper's peripheral vision. He lifted himself and the chair, then whipped in a circle, shoving one foot out. The hit grazed the mayor, sending him reeling. His angry shout rose to the ceiling. Jasper's momentum carried him into the table, where he crashed into the side, then tumbled across the room.

Barnhill hovered over him; then the muscular man joined him. The mayor waved the other man away. "Here I thought you might be helpful in order to save your lady love's life."

Everything in Jasper screamed a denial. Did they have Kinsley? "Don't touch her."

"I didn't want to. But her family keeps getting in my way. First her do-gooder dad, then her aunt Rhonda. She's the last bump in the road toward DC."

Rhonda's death hadn't been an accident. Neither had Willard Tuttle's. And her parents… Jasper shifted, the pain sending an ache down his stiff back. "You made sure Dean destroyed the accident report from Rhonda's death."

"Correction—the paperwork was misplaced. At least until all of this blows over."

"Murdering older folks who can't defend themselves? Rhonda Miller and Willard Tuttle trusted you. How do you sleep at night?"

"Very well, when meddling police officers aren't getting in my way." Barnhill thrust out a leg, catching Jasper's shoulder. Fire ignited at the sharp contact.

"What is this about, Barnhill? Why do you have it out for the Miller family?"

"They forced my hand, especially Rhonda Miller. God rest her soul."

Jasper clenched his jaw. "You made your own choices."

"As did she." Barnhill narrowed his eyes. "As did she." He paced the floor, then returned to stand over Jasper. The tip of one shiny shoe poked Jasper's arm. "Her aunt contacted me a couple weeks ago. That was an enlightening conversation. She told me one of my former employees overshared before his death. See, Rhonda volunteered at Tunnel Creek Hospice."

"The place you helped open," Jasper grumbled. "Hypocrite."

The foot on Jasper's arm pressed harder until he panted at the shooting pain.

Barnhill continued after a sigh, "Anthony Dixon used to work for me. He was a truck driver desperate for some extra cash, who transported weapons along the East Coast. Well, until his guilt got the best of him and he quit. Apparently, he couldn't keep his deep, dark secret any longer and decided to share what had happened with Rhonda Miller on his deathbed."

"'Deep, dark secret'?"

"Anthony Dixon is the man who crashed into Kinsley's parents' car. He was unhurt in the accident, and he was well compensated for the hit. By me." Barnhill paused, lips pursed in disgust. "It would've been much easier if they all died that day. Instead, Anthony survived and continued running weapons for another year or two while the Millers' daughter also survived and moved away, as you well know."

"So let me get this straight. This Anthony person had the goods on you, and he shared them with Rhonda Miller recently, before his death. And you couldn't take the risk of that getting out in the public."

Poor Kinsley. She'd spent years blaming herself for

her parents' deaths when it had been this monster's doing all along.

"Correct. Unfortunately, Mr. Dixon gave Rhonda Miller access to some unwelcome paperwork and pictures he'd taken of me through the years. You know. Contracts I didn't want shared. Pictures of me with people I didn't want to be photographed with." His face contorted into another crooked smile. "And Rhonda, in her wisdom—or shall we say, *stupidity*—contacted me before she turned them in to *you*."

Jasper clenched his eyes shut. If only she'd contacted him first...

"So you had Rhonda killed in what looked like an accident because she told you she had the file with the pictures. Why do you think Kinsley has them? Didn't you find the files at her house after her death?"

"Apparently, she must've realized after our conversation that she'd made a poor decision. She must've planned to mail them to her niece or lose them, so she'd placed the incriminating items from Mr. Dixon in her trunk before she died. My man on the job forgot to check her vehicle, and by then it was too late. Best I can figure now, a friend must've gone through Rhonda Miller's car and turned them into the funeral home director. Which we didn't know until you told Hammond you were headed there to retrieve those items."

"Let's not forget that you paid a desperate coworker to spy on Kinsley for you. To tell her some story about bats out here. Marta Akers."

Barnhill lifted his hands, a smug expression on his face.

Which confirmed Marta as an accessory.

Barnhill's gaze narrowed on Jasper. "Speaking of... Where is that file? I want all of it."

"It's in police custody. You'll never get your dirty hands on those pictures. Any of it."

Barnhill kicked Jasper's face and swore. Jasper turned just in time for the toe of the mayor's expensive shoe to graze his temple instead of his nose. Still, the impact made Jasper's eyes water and his throat catch fire.

Barnhill barked orders to the muscular man. Something about calling Hammond to retrieve the files from the station. *No.* Had Officer Anders placed Rhonda Miller's stolen paperwork in a safe place? Or…was Anders dirty, too? *Please, God. No.*

The urge to keep Barnhill talking took over. *Buy time.* Because with the way Barnhill was spilling his guts about his crimes, the man probably had a bullet with Jasper's name on it. "Why the weapons?" A metallic taste coated his tongue, making it feel thick and hard to speak.

"Why not? Do you know how much these weapons go for in other states? Enough money to live off for the rest of your life. Which for you, will be very short. But for me and the men helping me, it's enough money to fund a campaign that will get me into DC and pay Caruso and his friends." He motioned at the muscular man leaning against the wall a few feet away. "There are men all over the Eastern Seaboard desperate to get their hands on my guns."

"You are indirectly causing more crime by doing that."

Barnhill waved his hand dismissively. Jasper angled his head, staring up at Barnhill's flat brown eyes—eyes he'd once thought fair and caring. Now he knew better.

"Kinsley's parents? What did they do?"

Saying her name, especially in the company of such

terrible men, was an effort. Because all he could think of was her smile, how soft her hair felt when he'd embraced her and the way she'd fought through the last three days. Her strength and determination. Gutsiness. Her passion for animals and the kindness she showed to Gabe.

Lying on the floor of her parents' house, with death only inches away, Jasper could no longer deny that he still cared deeply for her, that he'd do anything to secure a second chance at whatever had started between them in high school.

Barnhill strode away, ignoring him. The mayor spoke quietly to Caruso, taking his gaze off Jasper. Jasper wedged his shoulders deeper into the floor so the ropes slackened. They'd loosened some but not enough. A movement behind the curtain in the back room caught his attention. He glanced that way and met Kinsley's rounded blue-eyed gaze.

He bit down on his tongue to keep from crying out. How had she gotten here? Noah's truck? How long had she been inside? Questions dominated his focus, but he shook them away and recaptured Barnhill's attention.

"Come on, Mayor. Fess up. Why did you murder her parents?" He hated doing this in front of her, but it was necessary.

Barnhill returned. Jasper quit wiggling the ropes around his wrist and pushed his features into a pained expression instead.

"Mr. Miller represented a man in Greenville who used to work for me. His name was Jack Sears. I fired Jack because he wasn't trustworthy."

"You mean he wouldn't do your illegal bidding, and it came back to bite you."

"We're done here!" Barnhill exploded, kicking Jasper in the stomach.

Nausea rose in his belly, and Jasper breathed in and out through his nostrils to keep from getting sick. *Please, God, keep her quiet. Keep her away from these men.*

"No," he gurgled. "*You're* done. You won't get—"

The mayor sent one foot flying again, and it caught Jasper in the temple. Maybe he wouldn't die yet. Not until he told Kinsley how he felt. Silver stars floated behind his eyes, and when he desperately tried to meet her eyes before blacking out, she was nowhere to be found.

# FIFTEEN

Kinsley slunk behind the thickets edging Whisper Mountain Tunnel's entrance. She'd learned the painful truth about her parents' murder from Barnhill's confession, then made her way to the tunnel once the men left with Jasper. She'd overheard their terrible plans for her and Jasper. Her legs shook. Branches scratched her cheeks, and a web stuck to her chin. She flicked it away and listened. Just like she had at her old house a half hour ago.

Once the men had driven off, she'd darted down the street, to the field she and Dad had used to cut through to a hiking trail in the forest. Noah's truck was parked behind a cluster of oaks, and she'd turned around. Driven back to the tunnel, parked the truck on a small service road nearby and snuck in here.

Kinsley closed her eyes briefly, her palms flat against the cold, rough rock wall. The pungent smell of thriving forest stung her nose. Dirt. Leaves. Tree bark. Moss. Water. All her favorite scents, part of God's creation. The outdoors. Fresh air.

Mayor Barnhill tainted this spot—this forest—for her. But he wouldn't get away with it.

How many years had she believed Mom's and Dad's

deaths were her fault? That their lives ended because she'd argued with them about her relationship with Jasper and Dad had been distracted because of her?

She curled her fingers until her nails indented her palms. It wasn't true. None of it. While the argument had been unfortunately timed, their deaths weren't her fault.

She swept her hands down her shorts, wiping off grit and prickers. If only she still had Jasper's loaner phone. They needed those pictures for evidence. But when she'd run away and hidden in the snake den, the cell must've slipped from her pocket.

She craned her neck. The mayor and his men must be inside with Jasper, because she hadn't seen them outside or on the trail leading up here. She'd heard their plan back at her house: Bring Jasper to the tunnel. Set up an explosive device that would go off when someone—*her*, they hoped—entered the hidden room. Killing and burying both of them in the process.

*Please, God, keep him alive. And help me do this.* She gripped the gun she'd retrieved from Noah's glove compartment.

She thought back to the frightening moment she'd entered her own house through the crooked cellar doors and had snuck up the basement stairs, the same way she'd played hide-and-seek with her dad and with friends during sleepovers. But when she reached the top of the stairs and snuck into the back room, she'd been shocked to find Jasper tied to a chair in the entryway, lying on the floor, and Mayor Barnhill standing over him.

Admitting his role in her parents' deaths.

Her stomach churned until nausea threatened. *Dad.* Had her mom known about the mayor's illegal activities back then, too? Maybe that was why Mom had been so stressed shortly before their deaths. And talk about stabbing Dad in the back. Her dad and the mayor had once been friends—or at least, close acquaintances. Together they'd voted to make Whisper Mountain Tunnel a historic site. How could the mayor traffic weapons through the very site he claimed to want to protect?

Kinsley forced herself into the tunnel. There wasn't time to dwell on the past now. She crept down its length for several yards. Déjà vu immobilized her muscles, and she sank into a ball on the cold, hard ground as fear swamped her and damp air choked her like that first attacker had days ago.

*God, please. I know You're here with me even though it doesn't feel that way. I'm sorry I've been mad at you for so long. Please forgive me. You protected me then, and You brought Jasper to protect me this time—well, and Sam the snake. Thank You.*

Kinsley pushed to standing, using the wall as a guide as she inched forward. Deeper and deeper she treaded. Gloomy darkness bled into the remaining light like ink. There. She located the area where she and Jasper had found the guns the other day. The heavy wood door was closed, but slivers of yellow light snuck in underneath it.

Kinsley inched closer to the door. Blood roared in her ears like she'd just sprinted a 5K.

"Is that thing rigged up yet?" Mayor Barnhill's voice.

"I'm working on it. There's a lot of wires here, boss."

Whose voice was that? The muscular man who'd been with the mayor at her house? They must be setting up the bomb.

An angry reply cracked the silence: "She won't fall for this."

Kinsley sucked in a shallow breath. *His voice.* Did Jasper mean her?

"Oh, she'll come here. And when she does, you'll both end up in so many pieces even Frank Anderson won't be able to make you look human again."

Kinsley shuddered. If she reached out, she could touch the door. But opening it also meant possibly tripping the bomb.

*Please, God, help me stop this.*

How could she distract the men without putting herself or Jasper in danger? She pushed the toe of her hiking boots around in the gritty dirt, then continued deeper into the tunnel, feeling along the walls. There had to be something she could do, a place to—

She squinted. Several feet from the hidden door, a section of the wall a couple-feet long dipped in, leaving an alcove. Grit and dirt clung to her fingertips as she inspected it. What if she hid inside, just enough to stay out of the men's direct line of sight?

A shout from the chamber sent a bolt of alarm up her spine. Was that Mayor Barnhill? No time to think about it. She fisted some pebbles from the ground, then threw them at the door. A couple went wide, but one tiny stone pinged on the mark. Then she tossed more, the popping sound louder this time. Backtracking, she slammed her back into the space, clasping the gun to her thigh, then flicked the safety off and held her breath. *Like riding a bike.* She smiled. *Thanks, Dad.*

The unmistakable creak of the door opening pushed the air out of her lungs. She lay as flat as possible in the alcove, the gun an unbearable weight in her grasp. Her chest heaved. What if this didn't work? How close were they to setting up this bomb?

Another question plagued her. Would Noah realize

something had happened because Jasper hadn't called or texted, as Noah had asked him to? *Please, God.*

Voices carried through the open door, interrupting her prayer.

"There's nothing. No one's here. I told ya, it was the rats."

"Go check the entrance."

Kinsley waited, her breath tickling her throat, as the *shush, shush* of footsteps sounded, the door shut and then the steps moved away. She inched her head far enough out and looked to her right. A blur of movement, then a large shadow filled her vision.

No! He'd faked going back inside.

"Look who I found."

Officer Hammond was part of this?

Kinsley lunged at him, swinging the gun full force. It whacked his forehead, and he let out a guttural shout of pain. She ducked and veered around him, her legs churning. Past the door to the hidden room. Did Jasper know Officer Hammond had betrayed them? *He must.*

A shout sounded as the man gave chase. She sprinted away, her chest bursting. Each stride sent her closer to the tunnel's entrance but farther from Jasper. Too late, she realized she never wanted to be far from him again. How could she ever consider loving anyone besides Jasper Holt? If she was honest with herself, no one else had measured up to him. She recognized that now. Admitted it. What she'd once considered a teenage crush was actually genuine affection. Steadfastness. Love. Love for that thoughtful, funny, caring man.

"Where you going, *Kinsley*?" Strong fingertips poked into her back, snagged a hold of her shirt. He yanked, but she swung her shoulder and dislodged his grip. She splashed through the shallow water collecting at the sides of the tunnel, kicking it back. Officer Hammond let out a frustrated shout but kept coming. He was only a few feet behind.

An oddly shaped figure stepped out from the edge of the entrance. The person was short of stature, and was that…?

Kinsley darted toward them, sliding in beside Elsa Tuttle and Sunshine, then turning to aim her gun at the attacker.

The older woman's faded blue eyes were hidden in shadow with the rising sun behind her, but the grim expression on her face was as clear as water.

Sunshine perched on her shoulder, his huge wings fluttering in anxious motions. Behind him, a man stepped forward, a dog at his side. *Noah and Dash.*

Mrs. Tuttle spoke to her bird, then looked behind her. "Let's get them out of our tunnel."

Jasper prayed Kinsley could outrun Dean Hammond. The thought of something happening to her—of losing her—sent a blade through his heart. He struggled against the rope around his wrists. It had loosened at her house earlier, and he rubbed it now against the edge of a large box that held the weapons. It wasn't sharp, but with enough friction, it might work.

Barnhill and the muscular man, Caruso, spoke in low tones to each other a few feet away. Only three boxes remained in the space, compared to a dozen from when he and Kinsley found the room yesterday. Where had the men relocated the weapons to?

"Go see what happened with Hammond," Barnhill demanded. "He should've been back." Barnhill let out an impatient epithet and strode over to Jasper as Caruso lumbered out of the chamber. "Get up. Out of my way. Go stand by the wall. It looks like I'll just have to set this bomb off myself."

Jasper stood and moved as he'd been told. "You're a coward."

"I've done things you'd never have the courage to do." Barnhill closed in, shoving him. Pressing Jasper's arms and hands into the jagged tunnel wall. A pointy rock struck his forearms, and relief cleared his vision.

A sharp edge. *Thank You, God.*

He rubbed the ropes against the jagged point. Slowly, so he wouldn't catch Barnhill's attention. Heat seared his wrist, and the rope's strength waned with each swipe across the stone.

Barnhill opened the box at his feet, rummaging through its contents. Then he let out a growl and kicked it.

"Did you forget the fuse?" Jasper mocked him.

The mayor charged forward, gripping Jasper's throat. "Here's what's going to happen. I'm going to get that woman in here. You two will be tied up. Together forever, right?" He sneered, and Jasper wheezed as his air supply dwindled. "Then my men and I leave, and this place will blow sky-high. Goodbye, tunnel. And the only evidence remaining will show that you were nosing around, having a romantic rendezvous, and accidentally set off an old explosive left over from the tunnel's earlier days. No one will be the wiser."

The ropes slackened completely, and Jasper's wrists pulled apart. He bunched his neck muscles tighter to try and draw in breath as the mayor's grip intensified. His lungs screamed.

*Now.*

Jasper dove forward, tackling Barnhill. They rolled to the ground in a messy pile, and Jasper gasped for breath as they wrestled. He pulled away, landing a solid punch to the mayor's face. Blood spurted from Barnhill's nose, and he howled in pained outrage.

In his peripheral vision, motion at the door meant someone else was entering. Bright light shone in. Jasper climbed off the mayor and struggled to his feet. The room spun. Something flew through the air, straight for Barnhill's staggering bent-over figure. The mayor let out a shriek as a large bird landed on his shoulder. What…?

"Jasper!"

*Kinsley!* Then she was there. She plowed into him, pressing her head to his chest. Her hair tickled his nose, proving she was real.

"Kins… You okay?"

"I'm here, Jasper. I'm fine. Are *you* okay?"

"I am now." He leaned into her, relishing the contact. The proof that she was safe. He settled an arm around her, holding her closer. "Don't leave."

"I won't, ever again."

Kinsley lingered at the ambulance's doors, her gaze following Jasper. Watching him breathe. Checking to make sure he was stable. The Tunnel Creek EMT vehicle was parked at a crooked angle in the Whisper Mountain Tunnel Visitor Center parking lot. Jasper dwarfed the stretcher as two EMTs took his vitals. He muttered at them, clearly irritated by all the attention.

Mrs. Tuttle sat on a bench at the parking lot edge, cooing to Sunshine. The bird side-eyed the entire scene, riled from the events of the last half hour. Across the lot, Noah spoke to Chief McCoy and two Tunnel Creek officers. Jasper's brother had notified authorities of Jasper's whereabouts once it became clear something had gone wrong.

As soon as the chief had arrived on scene, Kinsley told McCoy what she'd heard Mayor Barnhill say at her old house. Jasper had confirmed it, and they'd located Jasper's loaner cell by pinging its location. It had actually slipped out near the road when she'd climbed into Noah's truck the first time. Officer Anders had secured Aunt Rhonda's file and purse at the station, and he'd arrested Officer Hammond when he tried to force his way into the Records and Evidence room.

"Such a commotion, and I haven't had my coffee yet." Mrs. Tuttle scratched Sunshine's feathers just below his large beak. "I'm sure Jasper will be just fine, dear."

"I hope so." *Because I still love him.* She turned to the older woman. "How did you know to come to the tunnel?"

"My husband was a park ranger, you know. I still have Willard's radio. I heard a call come through about an altercation at the tunnel. It was Noah's voice, so I eavesdropped. Sunshine and I climbed right into Willard's truck and came down here."

Kinsley sank to her knees in front of the older woman. "I'm sorry you had to relive losing your husband through all of this."

"Well, now, I do believe justice was served, and I know *who* served it." She angled her gaze toward the sunrise. "I miss him so very much, but I will see him again. Maybe soon. We had many good years together. I'm grateful for that. Not everyone is blessed with so many happy years."

"I wish I could've known him."

"Oh, if you come visit me, I'll tell you all about him, and you'll feel like you did."

"I'd like that." Kinsley peered around. "I can't believe this happened, and it's over now."

"You know, one thing I've seen in my eight decades of life is that the Lord works His will in mysterious and mighty ways. Today is yet another example."

Kinsley nodded, her throat tightening. God had done all that *and* opened her eyes to the man she'd tried to forget. But…what if Jasper couldn't trust her again? What if he didn't feel the same about their love deserving another chance?

"Kinsley."

Jasper's familiar voice. Nothing on earth could stop her from turning to face him. He was half sitting up, still strapped down but definitely calling to her.

She stood. "I'll be right back, Mrs. Tuttle."

The woman smiled, deepening the wrinkles bracketing her face. "Take your time, dear. Sunshine and I will be just fine."

Kinsley hurried to the open ambulance doors. One of the EMT staff waved her inside, then jumped out. "You've got a couple minutes before we take him to TCGH."

She climbed in, and everything she'd planned to say to him disappeared like a turtle beneath a pond's surface.

"Are you hurt?" His gaze roved over her.

"I'm much better now." She inched closer, the urge to comb his mussed dark hair tempting. Instead, she grabbed the edge of the stretcher.

"Mrs. Tuttle," he murmured. "Is she okay?"

"She and Sunshine are safe."

"I can't believe that bird helped save me."

"You saved yourself. You got the rope off and took Barnhill out. Sunshine just moved things along when he and Dash threatened Officer Hammond."

"I can't believe it about Dean."

"Chief McCoy is pretty upset about the mayor's role in this, too. It's a huge shock to this small town."

"By the way…" He closed his eyes. "I'm sorry you had to hear all that at your house. About your parents. About how they died."

She drew in a slow, cleansing breath. "It was painful, but I'm grateful to find out the accident officially wasn't my fault." She touched his arm again, and his eyes opened. "I prayed earlier, asked God to forgive me for being angry at Him all these years. For being angry at myself."

"You're an amazing person, Kinsley." He drew his head back to gaze at her until a grimace gripped his features. She leaned over him, cradling his cheeks in her hands.

"What is it? What hurts?"

His eyes widened, and he slowly turned his face so he could kiss one palm. Then the other. Her knees wobbled at the tender gesture. "My heart sure doesn't anymore."

"What about your head?" She pressed a kiss to his forehead.

"Much better now."

When she pulled back, their eyes connected, setting the air on fire. She dropped her hands, twining them in a knot at her middle.

"I was so worried, Jasper."

"I could get used to you saying my name. You know, a lot. Every day."

"Jasper." She leaned in, pressing her head gently to his shoulder, breathing in his woodsy scent and thanking God he was okay. They were both okay.

"Atlanta is pretty far away." His voice cracked. "But I'm willing to—"

She set a finger to his lips. "Listen. Noah mentioned

a position that just opened in the park service for a wild-life biologist. I might have to travel around Sumter, but I could be based here."

"Here, in Tunnel Creek?"

"Yes." She smiled.

He let out a weak *whoop*.

"And then I can keep track of Sam."

"Sam?" He glowered at her. "Who's Sam?"

"Sam is a snake. He saved me, in that meadow on the backside of Whisper Mountain."

Jasper's dark eyes crinkled at the corners. "You have a snake friend?"

"I figure it's a start, right? I burned a lot of bridges when I left Tunnel Creek."

"I'm a forgiving guy." He patted his cheek.

She settled a quick kiss to it. "I'm so glad for that."

He patted his cheek again, right beside his mouth. "You missed a spot."

"Did I?" Her heart climbed into her throat, and she prayed the entreaty in her eyes spoke of what she felt for him. How grateful she was for their second chance. "Are you sure?"

"Completely sure."

"I am, too." She sealed them together in a tender kiss that forgave the past and set the course for their future.

# EPILOGUE

Jasper threaded his fingers through Kinsley's on the Jeep's console. She glanced his way, and they shared a smile in the twilight as Gabe jabbered from the back seat. A huge movie screen spread out in front of them, and a sea of cars surrounded theirs.

"I wanna watch the movie, Daddy. Do you want to watch it, Dash?"

The dog sat beside Gabe, his muzzle resting on the open window to sniff the spring air. Under the moonlight, the edge of Sumter National Forest painted the horizon shades of dark green.

Tunnel Creek Drive-In had never looked so picturesque, but all he could think about was the woman beside him.

Jasper glanced in the rearview mirror. His mom and Noah sat in Noah's truck behind them, unbeknownst to Kinsley. Brielle joined them in the backseat of the truck, wagging her eyebrows at Jasper.

When would the screen come to life?

"When's the movie gonna start, Daddy?"

"Soon, buddy." Please let it be soon.

"Miss Kinshley, can I have another piece of candy, please?"

"Here, sweetie." She pulled away from Jasper and poured a few more chocolate candies into his son's little palm, then offered him another sip from a juice box.

His nerves eased at her natural, maternal way with Gabe. Still, how would she react to this night? To what he was about to do?

Suddenly, the lights around the lot dimmed, and the big screen lit up. His heart pounded into a frantic rhythm as he squared his shoulders. *Here goes.*

He'd prayed for days, weeks about this day, planned out the details—and now, in the moment, he wasn't sure he could even speak correctly.

His face appeared on the screen, the bruises from that day in the tunnel long gone. In their place, Jasper saw a man in love, a man who'd lost a lot but gained so much more. A man who now had the woman who was his whole world living nearby, working with the animals she loved as a wildlife biologist with the local US Forest Service office, even finding and studying those elusive gray bats in the grist mill.

And a man who had braved letting a huge killer bird sit on his shoulder to show his devotion.

"Daddy! Is that you?" Gabe bounced around the back seat. "Why's that bird on you? Daddy, you're so big! Are you in the movie?"

"Jasper?" Kinsley turned to him, her soft blue eyes round pools of surprise. "You… Sunshine is… How did you… Did he…"

"I survived with both ears and nine fingers." He wiggled them, leaving one pinky tucked down for effect. She giggled, and he motioned her attention back to the screen. Hearing his own voice coming from the speakers was surreal and strange.

"I remember the day I first saw you in home economics. You sewed a circle around me and sewed yourself into my heart. The last few years, it was like a part of me had been missing." Sunshine lifted one foot and chewed on his ankle tag in the video.

"Daddy, the bird's eating his leg!" Gabe giggled. "He's gonna eat his leg!"

"Shh." He chuckled, but his gaze clung to Kinsley's profile as she stared at the screen with damp cheeks. He reached his right arm to cover her left hand with his.

The big-screen version of himself continued, "I let you go once, and I won't do it again. Don't ever think you're alone, Kins. You belong here—with me and Gabe, with my family. With this town. Tunnel Creek isn't home without you." His recorded self paused, gaining composure. Kinsley's other hand found his, gripping like her life depended on it.

"Kinsley Ann Miller, I believe God brought you back here for a reason. Please, will you do me the honor of marrying me? Be my wife and partner? Be Gabe's mommy? We both love you so much."

His huge image cut out, leaving a recent picture of them kissing under the mistletoe at his cabin at Christmastime. She reached across the cab and cradled one side of his neck. "Jasper, you brave, sweet man."

He closed his eyes as his son giggled, his family clapped and whooped, and neighboring cars honked their horns.

"Of course, I'll marry you and be Gabe's mommy. You two are my morning and my evening, and my everything in between. I don't ever want to leave you again."

"Yay, Miss Kinshley's gonna stay! Can we get a pet

snake?" Gabe interjected as Jasper leaned over to kiss Kinsley. "Like Sam?"

"Absolutely not," Jasper murmured against Kinsley's smiling mouth. Then he kissed his giggling fiancée to seal the deal.

* * * * *

Dear Reader,

Thank you so much for joining Kinsley and Jasper in Sumter National Forest! Although Tunnel Creek is a fictional town, it's based on a real place my family and I visited a few years ago. Walhalla, South Carolina, is the home of Stumphouse Mountain Tunnel, an unfinished railroad tunnel for the Blue Ridge Railroad in Sumter National Forest. We loved walking the tunnel's shadowy length and visiting the nearby Issaqueena Falls. It's a unique and beautiful place to explore, and I highly recommend going if you're ever in the area.

In Tunnel Creek Ambush, Kinsley and Jasper both carry around the burden of guilt from loss and from difficult situations in their lives. Guilt is something I've struggled with, as well. But God's word reminds us that because of Jesus, we are no longer to live in condemnation. We are to live as forgiven, consecrated children of God because of the finished work of the cross. I pray you remember that today and every day.

I love hearing from readers! Please look for me on Facebook (Kerry Johnson Author), Instagram or on my website, www.kerryjohnsonbooks.com, where you can sign up for my quarterly newsletter. God bless you and keep you!

Fondly,
*Kerry Johnson*

# Get 4 FREE REWARDS!

## We'll send you 2 FREE Books plus 2 FREE Mystery Gifts.

**FREE**
Value Over
**$20**

Both the **Love Inspired®** and **Love Inspired® Suspense** series feature compelling novels filled with inspirational romance, faith, forgiveness and hope.

---

**YES!** Please send me 2 FREE novels from the Love Inspired or Love Inspired Suspense series and my 2 FREE gifts (gifts are worth about $10 retail). After receiving them, if I don't wish to receive any more books, I can return the shipping statement marked "cancel." If I don't cancel, I will receive 6 brand-new Love Inspired Larger-Print books or Love Inspired Suspense Larger-Print books every month and be billed just $6.49 each in the U.S. or $6.74 each in Canada. That is a savings of at least 16% off the cover price. It's quite a bargain! Shipping and handling is just 50¢ per book in the U.S. and $1.25 per book in Canada.* I understand that accepting the 2 free books and gifts places me under no obligation to buy anything. I can always return a shipment and cancel at any time by calling the number below. The free books and gifts are mine to keep no matter what I decide.

Choose one: ☐ **Love Inspired**
Larger-Print
(122/322 IDN GRHK)

☐ **Love Inspired Suspense**
Larger-Print
(107/307 IDN GRHK)

Name (please print)

Address                                                                                                    Apt. #

City                                          State/Province                                    Zip/Postal Code

Email: Please check this box ☐ if you would like to receive newsletters and promotional emails from Harlequin Enterprises ULC and its affiliates. You can unsubscribe anytime.

> **Mail to the Harlequin Reader Service:**
> **IN U.S.A.:** P.O. Box 1341, Buffalo, NY 14240-8531
> **IN CANADA:** P.O. Box 603, Fort Erie, Ontario L2A 5X3

Want to try 2 free books from another series! Call 1-800-873-8635 or visit www.ReaderService.com.

*Terms and prices subject to change without notice. Prices do not include sales taxes, which will be charged (if applicable) based on your state or country of residence. Canadian residents will be charged applicable taxes. Offer not valid in Quebec. This offer is limited to one order per household. Books received may not be as shown. Not valid for current subscribers to the Love Inspired or Love Inspired Suspense series. All orders subject to approval. Credit or debit balances in a customer's account(s) may be offset by any other outstanding balance owed by or to the customer. Please allow 4 to 6 weeks for delivery. Offer available while quantities last.

**Your Privacy**—Your information is being collected by Harlequin Enterprises ULC, operating as Harlequin Reader Service. For a complete summary of the information we collect, how we use this information and to whom it is disclosed, please visit our privacy notice located at corporate.harlequin.com/privacy-notice. From time to time we may also exchange your personal information with reputable third parties. If you wish to opt out of this sharing of your personal information, please visit readerservice.com/consumerschoice or call 1-800-873-8635. Notice to California Residents—Under California law, you have specific rights to control and access your data. For more information on these rights and how to exercise them, visit corporate.harlequin.com/california-privacy.

LIRLIS22R3

# HARLEQUIN
## PLUS

Try the best multimedia
subscription service for romance
readers like you!

---

## Read, Watch and Play.

Experience the easiest way to get
the romance content you crave.

Start your **FREE TRIAL** at
www.harlequinplus.com/freetrial.